PSYCHIC
ZONE
MINDFIRE

The Psychic Zone

THE
PSYCHIC
ZONE
MINDFIRE

MATHEW STONE

Hodder
Children's
Books

a division of Hodder Headline plc

*With very special thanks to Andrew Beech and
Jonathan Goodwin*

First published in Great Britain in 1998
by Hodder Children's Books
A division of Hodder Headline PLC
338 Euston Road, London NW1 3BH

10 9 8 7 6 5 4 3 2 1

A Catalogue record for this book is available from
the British Library

ISBN 0 340 69836 5

Typeset by Avon Dataset Ltd, Bidford-on-Avon, Warks

Printed and bound in Great Britain by
Clays Ltd, St Ives plc

CONTENTS

1

Hit and Run

Dateline: New York City;
Saturday 31st March; 15.15.

'We'll never see each other again,' Sara Williams said
to her older brother, Joey. The pair of them were sitting
on the stoop of an old tenement building on Harlem's
West 129th St., sharing a bottle of Doctor Pepper.

'Sure we will,' Joey said confidently. Joey was
thirteen years old, a good-looking Afro-American kid
with a cheeky grin and bright, alert eyes.

'And how do you figure that one out? You lookin'
into the future again?'

'You know I can't do that.'

'That's not what Old Mother Henshaw in the downstairs apartment thinks,' Sara reminded him. 'She says
you have the second sight. She told me the other day
that you spook her out, the way you always know

1

what people are thinking without them ever telling you.'

'She gives me the creeps too,' Joey said uncharitably. 'She's always snooping around, wanting to know people's business. She's only been livin' in our block for the last coupla of years, yet she acts like she owns the place. And what's she doin' here anyway? I bet she could afford to live somewhere better than Harlem.'

'You bein' psychic again?'

'Nah,' said Joey. 'But she don't belong round here. You can tell it from the way she acts. Jeez, Sis, there ought to be a law against people like her.'

'That day her cat went missing, you knew where it was without even looking for it,' Sara recalled. 'And who else could have predicted that a third-rate team of no-hope losers from Peoria would win last year's Superbowl, 'cept for you?'

'They were just lucky guesses and hunches, that's all.'

'Sure.' Sara wasn't convinced. 'Here's my big brother with the chance to become the next Uri Geller, and he won't even admit it to himself.'

'Leave it out, will you?' Joey said awkwardly. He hated talking about the voices he kept hearing in his head. He hated the way he sometimes knew what everyone else was thinking. It made him feel different from all the other kids in the neighbourhood.

'So, if you're not psychic, how come you know we'll see each other again?'

'Loosen up, Sara, it's not like I'm blasting off for another planet!'

'It might as well be. Fat chance I'll ever get of going out-of-State, let alone to England.'

'Hey, if you don't want me to go, I won't.'

'What about Pa? Don't he have no objections about you leavin' home?'

'What does he care, as long as he can get his next fix?'

'It's not his fault,' said Sara, who always saw the best in everyone. 'He's fallen in with a bad lot ever since Ma died.'

Joey shuddered at the thought. He'd been there when his mom had been gunned down by a couple of hoods outside Lennox subway. The cops had come up with nothing, as usual. Said it had just been another mugging gone wrong, even when Joey had told them that the hoods hadn't taken their money. Heck, they hadn't even raised an eyebrow when Joey had said that one of them murdering muthas had spoken with a limey accent.

Joey could never forget that day. For one thing, it had been the day when his headaches had started real bad. It had been the day too when he'd started hearing the voices in his head.

'I never see Pa for days now,' he reminded her. 'You're the only person I care about, Sis. You know that, don't you?'

''Course I do,' Sara said. 'And sure, you've got to go. It's not every day kids like us get a chance like this.'

'And that Molloy broad said I could come back for the vacations,' he continued. 'This Institute in England

3

is gonna pay for my flights home.'

'Really?' Sara brightened up considerably. If she could see Joey every three months or so then maybe life in the New York slums wouldn't be so bad after all.

'Sure! Those guys are loaded! How else do you think they can come up with the bread to give me a place at one of the top private schools in the world? Hey, maybe I can sweet-talk Molloy into letting you come over and visit me!'

'That would be great!' Sara agreed. 'You want another Doctor Pepper?'

'Is Lisa Simpson yellow and cute?'

'Then go ahead and get me one as well.'

'Get 'em yourself!'

'Won't.'

'Aw, c'mon. Say, if I give you a coupla bucks then will you go and get them?'

Sara pretended to consider the matter. 'Can I get me a Snickers as well?'

Joey nodded. He dived into his jeans pocket and handed a couple of bills over to Sara, who took them and stopped at the edge of the sidewalk. There were no cars on the street, but she still waited for the traffic lights to flash the walk sign, before crossing over to the candy store on the other side.

Joey and his kid sister had been best buddies ever since their mother's death and now they were practically inseparable. Sometimes it was even as if they could tell what each other was feeling.

He was sure going to miss having her around, Joey

thought, as he watched her leave the store and cross back over the road with two bottles of Doctor Pepper.

Suddenly there was the sound of screeching tyres. A long black limousine – not the kind you'd expect round here – whipped around the corner. It headed straight for Sara. She turned, frozen to the spot.

'Sara!' Joey leapt up and screamed out a warning.

Too late. There was a massive *whump!* and the limo slammed straight into Sara. She was tossed into the air like a rag doll, tumbled over the car's roof, and landed with a dull thud on to the road.

Joey ran out into the road. He cradled Sara's head in his arms. But it was already too late. Sara was dead.

With tears streaming from his eyes, Joey looked after the hit-and-run limousine, which was already tearing around the corner. If he could only catch a glimpse of the number plate then at least he could get the cops to nail the maniac who had just gone and killed his sister.

Joey realised with a shock that there was no number plate. Whoever had killed Sara had wanted to make sure that there was no way they could be tracked down.

Joey raised his hands to his temples. There was a stabbing sensation in his head a hundred times more painful than any of his headaches. It was like his brain was about to explode. The world began to spin sickeningly around him and he fell to the ground.

His vision was becoming cloudy now, but Joey could just make out the back page of a newspaper which someone had tossed on to the sidewalk. There was a photograph there – of some businessman, he guessed. And a young white girl about his age. Short blonde hair. Impish face. Kinda pretty.

A rushing sound in his ears now, like that feeling he'd had when he'd seen his mom being shot. Forehead tingling. He was dimly aware of the sound of footsteps running towards him.

'Get an ambulance!'

'Is he OK? It looks as though he's in shock!'

'We've gotta do something! I coulda sworn I saw the girl move!'

'Nah. She's a goner! She didn't stand a chance!'

It's no good, Joey thought. *Can't you see? My sister, the one person in the world I love, is dead. I'll never ever see her again. My head is hurting so much. It's like it's gonna explode. My mind, it's so hot, feels like it's burning up, feels like it's on fire . . . Everything's so hot . . .*

And then, mercifully for Joey Williams, everything went black.

*Dateline: Heathrow Airport Terminal Four,
London, England;
Thursday 26th April; 07.05.*

Dr Margaret Molloy checked her watch and then looked up at the flight information screen in the busy Arrivals Hall. It was a little after seven o'clock and outside the airport building the weather was cold and grey. According to the overhead screen, BA Flight 174 from New York had just touched down.

Margaret Molloy was a kindly-looking woman who had just turned fifty. She was dressed in a sensible tweed suit and glasses, and wore her grey hair in a tidy bun.

As always, she had arrived at Heathrow much too early. She might have held several degrees in higher maths, but Dr Molloy always found it impossible to judge the driving time from staff quarters up at the Institute down to the London airport.

She'd already read and reread her copy of this morning's *Times*. Not much to interest her there. Just the usual stuff. Complaints about the latest education cuts. An irate letter from Disgusted of Islington about the latest on Channel Five. Even a short piece about a series of mysterious fires in the oil fields of the Middle East failed to spark any interest.

Dr Molloy still had half hour or so to wait until the New York arrivals came through customs and pass-port control. She tossed her copy of *The Times* into a nearby rubbish bin and passed her time studying the other men and women in the hall.

There was the usual collection of people waiting to greet friends and relatives off the plane. One tiny group of three men looked distinctly out of place, however. They appeared to be a little nervous, and were gathered together in a huddle. They seemed to be looking in her direction, whispering amongst them-selves. Dr Molloy immediately felt uncomfortable. Were they talking about her?

She walked over to the observation window which

looked down on to the tarmac. Down there Flight 174 was taxiing to a halt. She tried to catch a better look at the three men in the reflection of the glass.

Two of them appeared to be in their early forties and wore the smart uniforms of airline pilots. The third was much younger – probably in his mid-twenties, Dr Molloy guessed – tall and smartly dressed in a black suit. A Middle Eastern complexion. Maybe Egyptian or Iraqi, she thought. A tiny goatee beard. A cruelly handsome face. Dr Molloy frowned: he looked like the sort of person who would pull the wings off flies for the fun of it.

She watched the younger man walk up to the uni-formed official standing by the arrivals door. A brief conversation followed. It finished with the young man taking an ID card from his jacket pocket and flashing it in the airport official's face. Then the young man signalled to his colleagues, and the official stood back and allowed them through the arrivals doors.

Dr Molloy looked back down on to the tarmac. People were already leaving the aeroplane. She peered through her glasses and tried to spot Joey. She smiled, recognising the boy's bright red baseball jacket and cap. She looked at her watch: 7.15. She walked up to the arrivals doors and waited.

By 7.43, all the passengers from Flight 174 had streamed through the doors. There was no sign of Joey.

7.55: Dr Molloy started to get worried.

8.20: Dr Margaret Molloy somehow felt that she would never see Joey Williams again.

Dateline: Somewhere in England;
Thursday 26th April; 11.57.

Joey flicked his eyes open. He felt dizzy and he had the mother of all headaches. He reckoned that the foreign-looking guy and those other two prize creeps at Heathrow had gone and drugged him.

Well, they'd soon find out that it didn't pay to mess with him. On the streets of Harlem he'd been able to hold his own with guys twice, even three, four times, his size. Those bits of trash wouldn't know what had hit them.

Joey tried to sit up. He couldn't. It looked as though he'd been strapped down to some kind of bench.

On his head someone had placed a weird contraption, like one of the majorly cool power-helmets those guys on his favourite TV series wore. This helmet, however, was attached by numerous electrodes and wires to some pretty serious hardware: a bank of computers and overhead monitors, as well as stuff that wouldn't have looked out of place in the latest *Star Wars* movie.

One of the monitors showed a map of the world, like the ones he'd seen on TV pictures of Mission Control in Houston. Red lines criss-crossed the map like the veins in a butterfly wing, linking the Middle East to Europe, South America to the Indian Subcontinent, Antarctica to Africa.

The only light came from these monitor screens, but it was enough for Joey to make out his surroundings.

Judging from the high-vaulted ceiling, and the arched doorway to his left (which he could just see out of the corner of his eye), he decided he was somewhere underground. It reminded him of the subway tunnels back home – but it was way creepier. He could hear the constant drip-drip-drip of water from someplace far off. Rats scuttled in the darkened corners of the chamber. The grey pillars lining the walls were covered with elaborate stone carvings. Grinning gargoyles. Human-headed monsters. Devils with tiny pitchforks.

Joey heard footsteps echoing across the flagstoned floor. A woman's footsteps. They came nearer. A young woman's face peered over to look at him. Dark-haired and pretty, Joey thought, even though the green light from the monitors cast weird shadows on her face.

'Hi, Joey,' she said. She spoke with a slight accent. Joey tried to place it. Greek? Maybe even Middle Eastern, judging by her dusky complexion. Somewhere far away anyway.

'Who are you?'

'I'm Maria,' the woman replied and smiled – not a smile that instilled much confidence in Joey.

'Where am I?'

'With the Project.'

'What?'

'That will be enough, Maria,' another voice said.

This time the voice was male. English. Crueller and harder too. A man's face came in view. A gaunt, hook-nosed face, with narrow, green eyes. There was evil in those eyes, Joey knew. The newcomer was dressed in a lab coat the same colour as his snowy-white hair. A white surgical mask over his face concealed his identity.

'Is this the boy our agent told us about?'

'Yes, sir. Omar and his men brought him in an hour ago.'

'Omar?' asked Joey. 'That smart-suited mutha with his two thugs?'

The man in the white mask ignored Joey.

'Sir, are the restraints necessary?' Maria asked him. 'Surely the boy can do us no harm? If he knew of our purpose . . .'

'Go about your tasks, Maria,' White Mask commanded. Maria turned away meekly and disappeared from view.

White Mask bent down closer and Joey could smell the man's breath even through his mask.

'How are you feeling, Joseph Williams?' White Mask asked.

'Get lost, dog-breath.'

White Mask scowled. For one moment Joey thought that he was going to hit him. Then White Mask chuckled softly to himself.

'Such aggression! Such hatred! Sure fire!' the man said, and rubbed his hands gleefully. 'Our Project can put that to good use. Now, my young and fiery friend, it's time to work! The others in the desert sun proved too weak and fearful. They couldn't hold in check the powers they called into being. You, I trust, will be different.'

'Work? What sort of work?'

'Your mind is different to others, Joseph Williams.'

'What do you mean? Different? I'm the same as everyone else.'

White Mask ignored him. He knew that Joey was lying. 'And the power of your mind must serve the Project,' White Mask announced. 'The others were consumed in the Mindfire. You, I trust, will be different.'

'What others? What's the Mindfire?'

'You are nothing more than a tool, a tool to unlock the power of the earth,' White Mask said mysteriously. 'You will work for us. You will not ask questions.'

'And what if I don't want to do any work for you?'

White Mask turned round. Maria had left the room and wasn't there to hear him.

'Then, Joseph Williams, the Project will kill you.'

THE PSYCHIC ZONE

2

Hellfire

Dateline: Brentmouth Village, England;
Monday 7th May; Midnight.

The fox knew something was wrong as he made his way slowly towards the Institute. He felt it in every part of his being, from the points of his ears to the end of his white-tipped brush.

The old church clock of Saint Michael's down in the village had just chimed midnight. Up in the sky the moon shone brightly. Yet now the heat was almost unbearable, like those long summer days when the sun's scorching heat made his den hot and suffocating. But only hours ago the fox had been shivering on one of the coldest days in May he'd ever known. Where had this sudden heatwave come from?

Something was wrong.

Something was different.

The fox reached the top of the hill. He paused to catch his breath. It was getting hard to breathe: just as if all the oxygen in the air were being burnt up.

On other nights the fox would have turned tail and gone back to his den. But his vixen had just given birth to a new litter of cubs and they needed feeding. So, ignoring his fears, the fox slinked through the locked iron gates and passed a sign which read:

The Brentmouth Scientific Institute for Gifted Youngsters
Privately Funded with Government Assistance
Limited Scholarships Available
Headmaster: General A.C. Axford, OBE, M. Phil., B.Sc.

Lights blazed in several first-floor windows of the Institute. The two-legs there often worked late into the night. They posed no threat. The fox and his ancestors had never been caught on their nightly forages for food. They were much too clever for that.

The fox slinked round to the yard at the back. In the old days, before it had become a school, the Institute had been a country manor. This had been the old stable yard. Now the stables were gone, and a new kitchen annexe had been built on the site, along with several laboratories.

The fox sniffed the air warily. His nose tingled. Strange smells were on the breeze. Sharp, electric smells, unlike any he had ever known before.

Then he spied the black plastic bin-bags piled up against the kitchen wall. He grunted happily. Who cared what the two-legs were doing up in their laboratories? So what if tonight was hotter than a midsummer's day? All that really mattered was dinner!

Expertly he ripped open one of the bin-bags with his teeth and scattered the contents out onto the ground: slivers of burnt meat, scraps of paper, half-empty tin cans. He licked his lips and started to chomp greedily on the scraps of cooked meat and bones.

Kreeee . . .

The strange whining sound seemed to come from all around him. He looked up, eyes darting about: searching out the intruder in the dark.

No one was there. The fox was alone in the yard. After a few seconds the noise stopped. It must have been a passing owl or bat, on its own hunt for food. He returned to his meal.

Kreeee . . .

The fox stiffened and looked up again. It was louder now. Something was there after all! His ears twitched. He tried to locate the source of the shrieking noise. The red fur along his arched back began to bristle. Every muscle in his body tensed.

Wisps of smoke started to issue from the tumbled leftovers from the bin-bags. Scraps of paper crackled and crumpled, their edges turning yellow and then brown. The plastic bag smouldered and shrivelled. There was the unmistakable scent of burning on the night air.

Lights in the Institute's windows flickered, just as they would during an electrical storm. But this was no storm. This was something evil. This was something unnatural. Something *alien*.

The fox tried to run but it was no use. Even though the ground beneath his paws felt as hot as burning coals, his legs refused to move. Some invisible force enveloped him, taking control of his senses, burning him up from inside. Already his fur was singed. His flesh was scorched. Now his eyes started to dry up – turned to cinders.

Flames cascaded out of the fox's body, maggots of fire leaving a rotting corpse. Then the helpless, uncomprehending creature exploded in a ball of white-hot fire. It was all over in less than three seconds.

Of the fox there was no sign. No ashes. No bones. Nothing.

Except for a shadow on a wall.

THE PSYCHIC ZONE

3

A Shadow on a Wall

*Dateline: The Institute, Brentmouth Village,
England; Tuesday 8th May; 08.30.*

'Let's look on the bright side,' Marc Price said the
following morning as he inspected the still-smoking
ruins.

Marc was fifteen years old, a tall, wiry boy with a
shock of dyed blonde hair. He was wearing an old
Harley Davidson leather jacket, a pair of tatty jeans
and (non-designer) sneakers. Over his shoulder was
slung his backpack, containing what he'd managed to
complete of last night's homework before switching
on to the InterNet.

Rebecca Storm pulled back her long auburn hair,
which the morning breeze was blowing into her big
green eyes. She looked curiously at her best friend.
Then she turned back to the burnt-out shell, which

17

was all that remained of the Institute's kitchen.

Firemen were rooting around in the wreckage, looking for any clues as to the cause of the fire. Near them Sergeant Ashby and two of his local cops were making an unsuccessful attempt to stop Jean-Luc Roupie and Karl Petersen of Year Eight from checking out the damage. Liv Farrar from *The Enquirer*, the school newspaper, was busy taking photographs, pretending she was the Institute's very own Lois Lane.

'There's a bright side to the new kitchen annexe burning down then, is there?' Rebecca asked. She came originally from New York. Sarcasm was one of her specialities.

'Sure there is,' Marc replied cheerfully. 'With the kitchens zilched we'll be spared the biggest health threat known to man – old Mrs Chapman's school dinners!'

'Don't you think of anything else but your stomach?'

'Nope.' Marc turned back to the scene of the fire. 'Hey, Bec, you reckon it was arson?'

'Who'd want to torch the kitchens?'

'Anyone who tasted Chapman's stodgy spag bol last week. Forget the search for super-dense matter way up in space – you needn't look any further than the school diningroom.'

'Thank God I'm vegetarian then,' Rebecca said. 'It couldn't be arson anyway. The school grounds are protected by security cameras.'

'Don't I know it!' Marc sighed, remembering the time the cameras had caught him bunking off a particularly boring physics class. 'This dump is becoming more and more like a fortress every day.'

'It's what comes from having a Gulf War veteran as its Principal,' Rebecca chuckled. 'Anyway, nobody can get in or out without being caught on closed-circuit TV.'

'Nobody human, that is,' Marc said spookily. 'Didn't I tell you there'd be trouble if they built the new kitchen on the site of the old abbey?'

'Four hundred billion years of evolution and we end up with you!'

'What do you mean?'

'Marc, for a reasonably intelligent fifteen-year-old, you can be amazingly stupid at times!'

'We all know that centuries ago an old abbey stood on part of this site,' he reminded her. 'Maybe all those mad monks don't like their resting place being disturbed!'

'And maybe you need a brain transplant. You know as well as I do that there's always a perfectly rational explanation for everything.'

'I guess so. But my theory's much more fun!'

'There's the General. Perhaps he can tell us what happened.'

Rebecca pointed over to a gaunt, middle-aged, grey-haired man in a wheelchair who was chatting to one of the firemen. When he saw Rebecca and Marc he called them over.

'A tragedy,' he told them. His upper-class voice was clipped and precise: the voice of a military man. 'Mrs Chapman feels quite sick about it, of course . . .'

'I did tell her to lay off her own cooking,' Marc put in, not quite under his breath. Rebecca kicked him on the shin to tell him to shut-up.

'What caused the fire, sir?' she asked, and then added mischievously, 'Marc thought it was the work of ghosts.' Marc glared at her.

'I did not!' Marc looked at General Axford, who was scowling.

'If Mr Price persists in acting like a three-year-old, then his scholarship could quite easily be withdrawn.'

'Sorry, sir,' Marc mumbled. 'It was just a wild idea of mine, that was all. I guess I let my imagination run away with me sometimes.'

'Then we shall speak no more of it.' General Axford turned back to Rebecca. 'The fire was probably caused by a minor electrical fault. Shame I never dined there.'

'That's what you think!' Marc said.

'I'm sorry?'

'Forget it, sir.'

''Would have liked to have done, of course,' Axford said, 'But as soon as building work commenced, I was sent away . . .'

Rebecca nodded awkwardly and tried not to look down at the General's paralysed legs. She'd been working in one of the Institute's physics labs when the accident had happened. There'd been an almighty explosion in the grounds. The next thing she'd known, ambulances were milling around the staff quarters. Axford had been carried off on a stretcher to a private hospital somewhere down in London. When he returned to the school it had been in a wheelchair, and he had seemed slightly changed in some way.

'Worse things happened in the war,' Axford said, and for a half-moment there was a strange faraway look in his eyes. 'Lots of good men were lost in the desert out there . . .' He abruptly changed the subject. 'Let's be grateful that the annexe was built so far away from the classrooms and lecture halls.'

'Whatever happens, no harm must come to the Institute,' said a husky Germanic-sounding voice from behind Rebecca and Marc. 'It is the future. The future is all that matters.'

The three of them turned around to greet the newcomer. She was a tall and imposing woman, dressed – as always – in a stylish black jacket and skirt. She wore an unmistakable crisp and expensive-smelling perfume. Her blonde hair was cut short and, even on this dull and overcast day, she was wearing a pair of dark glasses.

'Right, as ever, Eva,' Axford smiled as the woman marched smartly up to his wheelchair.

Eva looked enquiringly at Marc and Rebecca. 'What are you doing here at the scene of this fire?' she demanded sharply. 'It is dangerous for young children.'

Before Rebecca could bridle at being described as a young child, Marc turned to Eva with a defiant look on his face. 'We wanted to see what had happened and if there was any way we could help,' he told her, not quite truthfully. 'The Institute is just as important to us as it is to you.'

Eva stroked her chin thoughtfully. 'Of course, it is,' she agreed. She smiled a smile which carried no sincerity whatsoever. 'Trust me, I'm just concerned about your welfare, that's all.'

'Eva takes a deep interest in all the students here at the Institute,' Axford reminded them both. 'And now we must take our leave of you.' Before they left, Eva glowered at Marc and Rebecca from behind her dark glasses.

'And you children should be at your lessons, instead of putting yourself in danger by wasting time looking at a pile of ashes, *ja*?'

'Er, yes,' Rebecca said. Eva nodded approvingly and then wheeled Axford away from the yard and up the driveway towards the main admin block. The wheels on his chair squeaked as he was pushed away.

'Cow!' Rebecca said, as soon as the two adults were out of hearing.

'Rebecca Storm!' Marc reproved her and laughed.

'Eva annoys me so much at times,' she said through gritted teeth. 'She always acts so damn superior to everyone. And she's only a jumped-up school secretary when it comes right down to it! And did she seriously expect us to believe all that stuff about being concerned for us?'

'She's got all of our best interests at heart,' Marc claimed.

'You seriously believe that?'

'Nope. Beneath that frosty exterior of hers there beats a heart of solid ice! When she gave us all that two days' holiday last term, you could have picked me up off the floor!'

'Yeah, that was a real surprise. And all to celebrate

the fact that the General was off the critical list. She'd never shown any sort of affection like that before.'

'Axford's changed ever since the accident,' Marc reminded her. 'He and Eva used to have an uneasy truce with each other. Now he relies on her more than he ever did before.'

'I know – and Eva loves it!' Rebecca said, and then turned back to the matter in hand. 'Anyway, so much for your theories of mad monks and arsonists! It was an electrical fire, that's all.'

Marc looked back at the ruins of the kitchen. The firemen and police were packing up now, and even Jean-Luc and Karl had moved off, although Liv was still clicking away with her Canon. Marc wandered over and Rebecca followed him.

'Remember the time I nearly blew up the chemistry lab?'

'A sulphur and potassium nitrate cocktail wasn't one of your best ideas!' Rebecca laughed. 'Even a physicist like me knows that!'

Marc gave her a friendly punch in the ribs. 'Hey, it was an accident!' he claimed. 'Anyway, we weren't in any real danger. I had a fire extinguisher standing close by.'

'Not that we needed it. The automatic smoke alarms and sprinkler system cut in and we all got soaked to the skin! My favourite Hamnett top was ruined and – Hey, wait a minute . . .'

'So why didn't the same thing happen last night?'

It was a good point. Rebecca knew it. She considered the possibilities. 'Perhaps the fault short-circuited the emergency systems as well? We had some problems last night up in one of the labs, too. I was working late with Simon Urmston on some experiments with electromagnetism.'

'I bet you were!' Marc said and winked suggestively at Rebecca.

'Marc, puh-lease! Simon is a pimply trainspotter who wears glasses and usually forgets to wash behind his ears. Now do you want to hear my story or not?'

'OK. Go ahead.'

'We experienced some fluctuations in the power supply. Nothing too serious. But it did throw some of our experiments off.'

'Exactly when did this happen?'

'Round midnight, just before the fire.'

'Now that is interesting. I was up late last night in the boys' hostel, working on my PC.'

'Fooling around on the Net, more like.'

'And at about the same time, I crashed,' he said. 'Just when I was downloading this really cool game.'

'You think there's some connection?'

'It could explain why the sprinkler system didn't work.' He knelt down to inspect a portion of the outer wall which had survived the fire. 'But it wouldn't explain this.'

Rebecca joined him by the wall. Etched on the concrete at floor-level there was a blackened image. It reminded her a little of cave paintings she'd seen in south-western France.

'What is it?'

Marc placed his hand against the image and then

quickly withdrew: it was warm to the touch.

'It looks like the shadow of an animal,' Rebecca said. 'A fox, maybe, or a dog.'

'Now who's in need of a brain transplant? How can a fox leave its shadow on a wall?'

'I've seen something like this before,' Rebecca said slowly, and stood up. 'Last year I went with Mom to a conference just outside Hiroshima.'

'Where they exploded the first nuclear bomb?'

'That's right. The bomb was so powerful that people near the centre of the blast were disintegrated. Nothing of them remained. Nothing, that is, except their shadows, which had been burnt on to the walls – ' Rebecca looked back at the image of the fox – 'exactly like this.'

'Hang on a minute,' Marc said, as he tried to follow her reasoning. 'You think that this shadow was produced by some massive charge of energy, like the heat from a nuclear bomb?'

'I didn't say that.'

'It might just have escaped your notice, Bec, but no one's been nuking Brentmouth recently! Least not so's I've noticed.'

'I know,' Rebecca said, with a wry smile. 'But something produced that shadow. It wasn't there yesterday.'

'You can't be serious, Bec. The amount of heat needed would have to be – '

'About three hundred million degrees,' Rebecca told him. 'Whatever produced this shadow was twenty times hotter than the sun!'

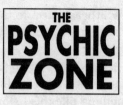

THE PSYCHIC ZONE

4

The Legend of Sister Uriel

Dateline: The Project; Tuesday 8th May; 09.55.

'Joey? Are you all right?'

Joey opened his eyes and remembered where he was. His head was aching and his entire body felt weak, as if all the energy had been drained out of it.

'Joey, are you all right?' the voice came again.

Joey's eyes focussed. Maria was standing over him. She placed a hand on his wrist and checked his pulse. Then she made a note on the clipboard she was carrying.

'What happened?' His lips were dry and cracked. He found it difficult to speak.

'You passed out, that's all. Don't worry – the blackouts will get shorter and shorter in time. They did with the others.'

'Others? Which others?'

'Never mind.'

'My head hurts.'

'That's the side-effect from creating a Mindfire,' Maria reassured him. 'That'll pass in time too.'

'Mindfire?' Once again that strange word. The same word White Mask had used. 'What do you mean?'

'I can't see any harm in telling you. The Mindfire is the product of your inner – '

'That will be all, Maria. Return to your duties.'

Shoot! Joey thought. White Mask had returned, and just when he was going to find out exactly what he was doing here.

'Sir, he's only a child. He's confused, scared – '

Scared? Joey thought indignantly. *No way am I scared, lady!*

'His feelings are of no concern to me,' White Mask said.

'Then they should be, sir. His emotions are interfering with the Mindfire, making it unstable. The others were frightened and remember what happened to them.'

'Several oil fields accidentally set alight in the Middle East,' White Mask said, casually. 'A minor example of what the Mindfire is capable of.'

'The children who tapped into the Mindfire died, sir,' Maria said, daring to bring a suggestion of recrimination into her voice. 'They were burnt alive by the very same forces which they had brought into being.'

'Then let us hope that Joseph Williams can control the Mindfire better than they can.'

'We were lucky that last night's fire didn't spread too much and that the fire service arrived in time. But if Joey knew of our purpose, we could tune his talents much more finely.'

'You were employed by the Project as a nurse,' White Mask reminded her.

'I know, sir – '

'Your concern is for the boy's physical well-being, not his psychological welfare!'

'I'm sorry, sir.'

Joey heard Maria's footsteps echo away into the distance.

'You get your kicks picking on women as well as young kids, then, do you?' Joey asked with a sneer when Maria had gone.

'Do not provoke me, Joseph Williams. For the moment you serve our purposes.

'*Our* purposes?'

'We are called the Project,' White Mask said. 'That is all you need to know. And – I might add – more than most people on this miserable little world have a right to know.'

'And it was your guys who met me off the plane from JFK? And took me to – ' Joey looked around at his surroundings and the ugly stone carvings on the walls – 'say, where are we anyway? The Chamber of Horrors?'

'That is no concern of yours.'

'Let's see, somewhere underground, right?'

Joey thought back to the journey from Heathrow Airport. He'd originally thought the three men with airside passes and official-looking IDs had been plain-clothes cops. They'd certainly looked mean enough. It was when they'd blindfolded him and bundled him into the back of that unmarked van that he'd realised that they were no such thing.

The journey had taken all of two hours, travelling at, he guessed, fifty miles an hour. Flight 174 had touched down in the morning, so the sun had been in the east. The van had had darkened windows but Joey remembered feeling the sun on the right side of his face for most of the time.

'I reckon we're about a hundred miles north of London.' He chuckled to himself when he saw the surprised look in White Mask's eyes. 'In fact, pretty much near the Brentmouth Institute.'

'Perhaps.'

Joey groaned theatrically. 'C'mon, give me some credit! So why pick this place? What's so special about Brentmouth?'

'I have my own reasons,' White Mask said. 'You are a very clever child, Joseph Williams.'

'Sure I am,' Joey replied. 'And less of the child, buster! I'm thirteen-and-a-half years old, and, as far as I'm concerned, that makes me more than a match for anyone!'

Dateline: The Institute; Tuesday 8th May; 14.15.

'You see, I told you it's impossible,' Marc said smugly, as Rebecca passed a Geiger counter over the shadow on the wall. She'd borrowed the instrument from the physics lab, telling Mr Boyle that there was private research she wanted to do.

'It's no more impossible than your theory of mad monks,' Rebecca retorted. She frowned. The portable Geiger counter was emitting none of the tell-tale crackles that indicated the presence of radiation. She clicked the machine off and stood up.

'You're really worried about this, aren't you?' Marc said when he saw the grim look on her face.

'I don't like mysteries, Marc. Something gave off so much heat that it made that shadow. I want to find out what.'

'Could the Geiger counter be faulty?'

'I've never had any problems with it before.'

'Then this shadow couldn't have been produced by a blast of thermonuclear radiation.'

'What could have caused it?' Rebecca checked the Geiger counter once more. There was no doubt about it. It was working perfectly.

'You won't find anything with that.'

Rebecca and Marc looked up at the young girl who was standing at the far end of the yard, watching them. She was slim and pretty, with large blue eyes. Her blonde hair was tightly cropped, which she thought made her look like a tomboy, but which actually made her appear younger than her thirteen years. She spoke with a slight local accent, which several years' coaching by her private tutor hadn't quite erased.

'And what makes you think that, Colette?' Marc asked.

'All your fancy gadgets won't tell you how that thing got there,' Colette said and walked over to them, her hands rammed into the pockets of her jeans. She knelt down to examine the shadow on the wall. 'Spooky, isn't it?'

'Told you so,' Marc whispered to Rebecca. Rebecca ignored him.

'What are you doing here, Colette?' Rebecca asked her. 'General Axford doesn't like non-students hanging around the Institute.'

'When your dad's company owns the grounds you can do what you want,' Colette said with a grin. 'I saw the fire last night from Fiveways. I wanted to take a closer look. Father Kimber was coming here this morning so he offered me a lift.'

'Kimber?' Rebecca asked. The name was unfamiliar to her.

'Emmanuel Kimber, the new priest up at Saint Michael's,' Colette explained. 'A sweet guy. Took over last month from old Matthews. He was round at our place asking for donations.'

'Why would he want to visit the Institute?' Rebecca wondered.

'Who knows?' Colette said with an indifferent shrug of her shoulders which really meant: *who cares?*

'Maybe he wants your headmaster to contribute to the church funds as well.'

'He'll be lucky,' Marc said. 'Axford isn't religious. He doesn't believe in anything that can't be proved by scientific observation.'

'This is much more interesting,' Colette said. She examined the shadow more closely. 'What do you think caused it?'

'Thermonuclear energy!' Marc laughed. Rebecca glared at him.

'Ghosts!' Rebecca said. 'Or at least that's what Marc thinks!'

'Sister Uriel, then,' Colette said and nodded wisely.

'I beg your pardon?'

'It's an old legend in these parts. 'Course neither of you would have heard of it, not coming from round here.'

'Heard of what?' Marc wanted to know.

'Three hundred years ago part of the old abbey burnt down – the revenge of Sister Uriel.'

'And who was she?' Rebecca asked.

'Some nun who was having an affair with the abbot of a nearby monastery in the 1600s.'

'Two old abbeys in one tiny village?' Rebecca asked. 'Isn't that unusual?'

Colette shrugged. 'Not round here,' she said. 'There are loads of old churches and holy places in this part of the country. Stand on the top of the Darkfell Rise and you can see at least seven or eight, all in a line. Sometimes I think they were all planned that way.'

'So where was the monastery built?'

'No one knows. It was destroyed when Henry VIII tore down all the monasteries.'

'Tell us more about Uriel and her abbot,' Marc urged.

'When their secret was discovered, they tried to escape through an underground passage which linked the abbey and the monastery. The abbot got away scot-free and was never heard of again.'

'Men are pigs,' Rebecca said, with feeling.

'Uriel was killed for being a witch. At least that's what they say. But a hundred years later her ghost returned to burn the abbey down to the ground.'

'And now she's back!'

'Grow up, Marc,' Rebecca snapped.

'As I said, it's just a story,' Colette said, although it was clear that she half-believed in the tale at least. 'For years afterwards people around here called this the most haunted place in England.'

'This is the present day!' Rebecca reminded them, even though she felt an irrational shiver of fear run down her spine. 'And every sensible person knows that there are no such things as ghosts.'

'There's evil here, though, I can feel it,' Colette said. 'Some people say that there are miles of tunnels underneath the Institute – all that remains of the old abbey. We don't really know what might be down there. Maybe even Sister Uriel . . .'

Rebecca sighed and raised her eyes heavenwards. Colette was being far too melodramatic. What was more, Marc was lapping it all up! She watched as Colette bent down to touch the mysterious shadow on the wall. Suddenly the girl swayed uncertainly. Marc was at her side in a second and helped her to her feet.

'What is it, Colette?'

'I felt dizzy for a moment, that's all,' she replied, shrugging him off. Colette hated having to rely on anyone. She raised a hand to her brow. 'Are either of you hot?'

Rebecca and Marc each shook their heads.

'Maybe you're coming down with a fever?' Rebecca suggested. 'I could take you to the sick bay. I'm sure Nurse Clare would bend the rules a little and see you.'

'I'll be fine.' Colette stretched out her arms and yawned.

'Too many late-night parties?' Rebecca asked, enviously. With the amount of homework she and Marc were given, she hardly ever went out partying.

'I've been having problems sleeping lately, that's all,' Colette told her. 'Nightmares and things. Ever since Dad and I came back from that business trip to New York.'

'Talking of nightmares, I'm going to have to finish my chemistry assignment before last class today,' Marc said, looking at his watch. 'Now why couldn't Uriel have burnt down the chemistry lab instead?'

'What kind of nightmares, Colette?' Rebecca wanted to know.

Colette frowned. She didn't like to admit to many weaknesses, and she felt uncomfortable talking about it.

'There's one in particular. I keep dreaming about a

traffic accident. At least, I think it's an accident. A young black girl. About my age. Knocked down by some kind of fancy car. A Merc, maybe, or a limo. I can still hear her big brother's screams in my mind – as though he's somewhere really, really near...'

THE PSYCHIC ZONE

5

The Ball of Fire

Dateline: The Institute;
Wednesday 9th May; 12.45.

'Don't you think you're taking this nun business a little too far, Marc?'

Marc was working at one of the PCs in the Institute's library. An untidy pile of disks was scattered in front of him. Apart from Marc and Rebecca, the library was empty. It was lunchtime so most of the Institute's students were spending the time in one of the school's several commonrooms.

'Call it historical research, Bec.' He inserted a disk into the machine. 'I want to see how true Colette's story is.'

Rebecca peered over his shoulder. 'What exactly is it you're doing?'

'This disk is a floptical – '

'A what?'

'A floptical. It holds as much data as a CD, but you can actually write and rewrite to it.'

'So what's on it?' Rebecca asked. She watched Marc download a file named 'Index' on to the hard disk and open it up.

'Stuff from the local parish records.'

'Why should something like that be in a science library?'

'It's part of some socio-historical project Axford is working on, as a favour for Miss Rumford over at the local folklore society. With a bit of luck there should be a mention of our Sister Uriel on this.' He tapped in the nun's name, called up the find facility, and then frowned at the information on-screen.

'Urmston, Simon?'

'You've got the wrong disk, idiot! That's a register of everyone at the Institute.' Rebecca sniggered and reached over his shoulder and scrolled down to a name she didn't recognise.

>WILLIAMS, JOSEPH. MATHEMATICS MAJOR. PERSONAL TUTOR: DR M. MOLLOY

'That's odd. I'm doing math subsid and I've never heard of him.'

'You should have. According to this, he was awarded a scholarship about a month ago.'

'Maybe he decided not to take it up?'

'What does it matter? He's not the one we're interested in.' Marc shrugged, closed down the file, and ejected the floptical.

'I will take that,' said a familiar voice behind them.

A hand reached over Marc's shoulder and long power-ful fingers snatched the disk from him. He smelt that familiar, crisp fragrance.

'Er, sorry, Eva.'

The six-foot blonde stared down at him through her dark glasses. She had sneaked up on them as silently as a big cat stalking its prey. It was something Eva did particularly well.

'Why are you so interested in the Institute's register of students?' Eva asked.

'It was a mistake. I got the wrong disk.' Marc wasn't sure that Eva believed him.

'People can be *too* curious, here, at our Institute,' Eva said. She tapped the disk thoughtfully against her chin.

'I thought that's what being at the Institute was all about,' Rebecca said defiantly. 'Asking questions, being curious. That's what General Axford always tells us.'

'That is what the General says, yes,' Eva said. She smiled frostily at them and then turned and marched out of the library.

'The General's not going to be happy if she tells him we've been rooting around in the school records,' Rebecca said.

'Relax, Bec.' Marc inserted the correct disk into the PC. 'It was a perfectly innocent mistake.'

'And what did she mean? "People can be *too* curious",' Rebecca wondered, but Marc wasn't listening. He let out a whoop of triumph.

'Wait till you get a load of this, Bec!' he crowed. He read out the entry displayed on the screen.

'For acts most contrary to the Laws of our Sovereign Lord, Jesus Christ, and for showing contrition neither great nor small, Uriel was condemned to the eternal flames of Hell. She was sentenced to be incarcerated until the end of her days. As the final stone was laid over her chamber —'

'They buried her alive,' Rebecca realised. She shuddered. 'I didn't realise how barbaric they could be back in those days.'

Marc continued. 'As the final stone was laid over her chamber, she swore undying revenge unto the abbey and the grounds thereof. "Ye who send me to perdition, be ware that the flames of Hell shall come to burn ye all," the witch said. She vowed that she would return, swathed in the eternal all-consuming flames of Hell itself, every hundred years, on the unholy feast of Beltane, until the end of all time.'

Rebecca shivered. 'It's just coincidence.'

'Uriel did die four hundred years ago and the place did burn down exactly a hundred years later in the 1700s,' Marc pointed out.

'Coincidence,' Rebecca said once more. 'And you've no proof that there was another fire a hundred years after that.'

'We're no proof there wasn't.'

'And what's "the unholy feast of Beltane" when it's at home anyway?'

'The greatest occult festival of the year after Hallowe'en. April 30th. They used to burn bonfires then to ward off evil.'

'Then Uriel's a hopeless time-keeper,' Rebecca said.

'We're already a week into May. So much for your ghostly theory!'

Before Marc could remind her of her own failure in coming up with a convincing explanation for the fire and the shadow on the wall, all the lights in the library went out. The PC cut out and its screen went blank.

Rebecca looked out of the window. The lights in the other windows of the Institute had failed too.

Kreeee . . .

'What is it? Where's it coming from?' Rebecca asked. Both she and Marc looked around the library, searching in vain for the source of the high-pitched whining.

Kreeee . . .

The lights switched themselves on again. The PC buzzed back into life. The whining sound vanished as mysteriously as it had appeared.

'Maybe Axford forgot to pay the bill?' Marc suggested nervously. He checked the file he had been reading. It seemed to be undamaged.

'That was the second power-cut in two days,' Rebecca remarked.

She turned around as she heard the library door open. Colette was standing there, a worried look on her face.

'Colette, what are you doing here?' Rebecca asked.

'One of the kids outside told me you were here. There's something outside I think you'd better see . . .'

Rebecca and Marc followed her out of the library. They went down the stairs, past the noticeboards pinned with the usual boring announcements and out into the yard.

A small ball of flame was hovering several inches above the ground. It was a white-hot globe of blazing energy, crackling and spluttering in mid-air. The light it was giving off was so bright that they had to shield their eyes. They felt its scorching heat on their faces.

'What is it?' asked Marc.

'It's smaller now,' Colette said. 'A minute ago it was the size of a football.'

Even as they watched, the fireball shrank until it was little more than a floating pin-prick of light, although the heat it gave off was still just as intense.

Kreeee . . .

The fireball blipped out of existence. Rebecca rushed to the spot where it had been.

'There's a perfectly natural and scientific explanation for this,' she said. She was trying to sound calm but wasn't being very successful.

'There is?' Marc asked. 'Just as there's an explanation for that shadow?'

Rebecca examined the patch of ground over which the fireball had been hovering. It was blackened and scorched. But the surrounding area seemed strangely unaffected. There were some scraps of litter nearby. These too showed no sign of having been touched by the fire.

'It could have been ball-lightning.' Rebecca was clutching at straws now, and both she and Marc knew it.

'On a day like this, without a storm cloud in the sky?' Marc asked.

Colette had wandered off to a corner of the yard

and she called them over. She was kneeling down and inspecting something she had found on the ground. She made to pick it up.

'Careful, it might be hot!' Rebecca warned.

'It's OK.' She handed her discovery to Marc, who turned it over thoughtfully in his hands. It was a molten lump of metal, hard and greyish-white in colour.

'You're the chemist,' Rebecca said. 'What do you make of it?'

'I'd have to run a couple of tests on it up in the lab, but I'd guess it's tungsten.'

'What's it doing out here in the yard?' Rebecca asked, but Marc was no longer listening. He turned back to her. There was a worried expression on his face.

'Bec, tungsten has the highest melting point of any metal,' he said. 'You'd need over three thousand degrees to knock it out of shape. But something's melted this like it was butter.'

'Not all of it,' Colette corrected him. She took the lump of tungsten and turned it over. 'See this smooth, straight bit in the metal there – and this other bit which crosses over the first bit. What does it remind you of?'

'A cross,' Marc said. 'A cross belonging to a nun . . .'

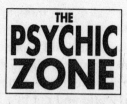

THE PSYCHIC ZONE

6

Who is Joseph Williams?

Dateline: The Institute;
Wednesday 9th May; 13.15.

'Don't be ridiculous,' Rebecca said curtly. She turned the lump of metal over in her hands and examined it, before handing it back to Marc. 'It's just coincidence that part of the metal has melted down into the shape of a cross.'

'So do you put that ball of fire down to coincidence as well?' Marc asked. '"The all-consuming flames of Hell". That's what the old records said.'

'I'm not going to give in to any of your mumbo-jumbo, Marc Price.'

'Go and ask one of your teachers,' Colette suggested. 'They're all supposed to be so smart.'

Rebecca shook her head. 'No, I'm going to solve this mystery myself. After all, I'm a scientist.'

'That's not the real reason though,' Marc said and grinned. 'Is it, Bec?'

'Of course it isn't!' she said superiorly, and turned to Colette. 'I want to prove to Marc just how wrong he can be! I want to show him once and for all that we're living in the real world and not in a Hammer horror movie or an episode of *The X-Files*!'

'Rebecca has no sense of romance,' Marc announced to Colette. 'There is one other thing that's worrying me though.'

'If I were you I'd have more than just one other thing to worry about!'

'Be serious, Bec. What's a lump of tungsten doing out here in the yard?'

Rebecca's eyes narrowed. That thought had bothered her as well.

'Maybe it's from one of the chemistry labs?'

Marc casually tossed the tungsten into the air, catching it as it fell. 'We don't keep this much in the labs,' he told them both. 'We'd have no need for it.'

'So what is it for?' Colette asked.

'Tungsten's used as the filament in electric light-bulbs, amongst other things,' Marc informed her.

'Amongst what other things?'

'It's also used as an alloy in things like armour-plating or missiles in wartime.'

'Gross,' said Colette, who hated fighting of all kinds.

'Yes, it's gross.'

Marc threw the lump of metal into the air again and caught it.

'It's prized because of its heat-resistant properties.'

'Qualities it didn't display here,' Rebecca realised. 'Marc, what's this to do with that shadow we saw on the wall?'

'Two blasts of thermonuclear heat in two days,' Marc said. 'Heat which seems to come from nowhere.' He threw the tungsten into the air for a third time and watched the sun glint on its greyish surface. Then he frowned.

'Two blasts of what *seem* to have all the properties of thermonuclear heat,' Rebecca corrected him. 'If it really was, we'd all be atomised by now.'

'And I bet you'll find no trace of radiation again if you tried your Geiger counter test now.' Marc threw the lump of metal into the air for a fourth time.

'Marc, will you stop playing with that! You're driving me nuts!'

'Watch,' he told both of them. He tossed the lump of metal into the air again, and caught it on its descent.

'So you're going to be trying out for baseball practice this term,' Rebecca said, unimpressed.

'Bec! Cricket in England! Now both of you watch more carefully. See what happens to the ball at the apogee.'

'The what?' asked Colette.

'The top of the throw,' Rebecca explained. 'Marc likes to show off with big words sometimes. It's his way of compensating for his minuscule personality.'

Marc ignored the jibe. 'Take a look at it the moment before it starts to fall to earth,' he said. He tossed the ball of metal into the air once more.

Rebecca and Colette watched it rise, and then, just for one quarter of an instant, it halted in mid-air and hovered, exactly like the ball of fire they'd seen earlier. Then it fell back down into Marc's out-stretched palm.

'See what I mean?'

He threw the tungsten into the air again. This time, however, he wasn't able to catch it. As it reached the top of the curve, some force seemed to deflect it. It was as if a massive wind had blown the heavy lump of metal off-course. But there was not even a breeze, and the leaves in the trees of the Institute grounds remained still.

The lump of metal thudded to the ground a couple of metres away from them. Marc went over to pick it up, and then glanced in the direction the metal had been deflected.

On the other side of the yard, past the police and fire brigade signs saying 'Keep Out', the shadow on the wall seemed to be looking defiantly at him.

'What happened?' asked Colette.

'Something was attracting it to the site of the fire,' Marc told her.

'Attracting it?' Colette repeated. 'You mean, like a magnet?'

'Could be.'

'Well, is that so strange?' Colette asked.

'Do you see anything even vaguely looking like a magnet?'

'And there's just one other little problem as well,' Rebecca said thoughtfully.

'Bec's right,' Marc told Colette. 'Tungsten isn't naturally magnetic.'

'Perhaps there's some iron ore in it?' Rebecca suggested.

'Maybe,' Marc said, and slipped the lump of metal into his pocket. 'We'll know after I've run those tests.'

'Too many questions and not enough answers,' Rebecca said. 'Marc, do you think we ought to tell General Axford about all this?'

'I thought you wanted to prove me wrong all by yourself?' he teased.

'But this could be serious,' Rebecca continued. 'First the fire in the kitchens and now all this. The Institute could be in danger.'

'Let's do some investigating ourselves first, before we tell Axford,' he said. 'Otherwise you know exactly what'll happen. He and Eva will take charge of everything, and we'll never get to find out what's been going on.'

Rebecca wasn't so sure, but finally she agreed. She looked at her watch. 'I've got to run off to my math class.'

Marc looked at his own watch. 'You've got another twenty minutes or so,' he told her. 'What's the big rush?'

'There's something I want to ask Dr Molloy,' she said.

After she had gone, Colette turned to Marc. 'You really do think that ball of fire had to do with Uriel, don't you?' she asked.

'I'm not quite sure,' he said truthfully. 'But I do

know that there are some things which can't be explained away by all of Rebecca's scientific equations.'

'Like ghosts?'

'Maybe.'

'You surprise me,' she said.

'Surprise you? Why?'

'I wouldn't have thought a science student like you would believe in things like that.'

'I didn't say I did,' Marc put her straight. 'But I've an open mind. Scientists are treating seriously things which only a few years ago they thought were superstition. Stuff like UFOs and the paranormal and ESP.'

'Sometimes I think I hear a voice,' Colette admitted a little sheepishly.

'You mean in those dreams you were telling us about?' Marc asked. 'If you're still having trouble sleeping at night you really ought to see a doctor.'

'No,' she said awkwardly. 'I hear it when I'm awake. But when I turn around there's no one there.'

'What kind of voice?' Marc asked.

'I don't really know. It's not like I hear it with my ears, but in my head. But that's stupid, isn't it? I've been hearing it more and more recently . . .'

For some reason he wasn't quite sure of, Marc found himself glancing back at the spot where the fireball had appeared, and then at the fox's shadow on the wall. He was about to question Colette further when the young girl gave him a nervous smile.

'Anyway, it's probably just my imagination.'

'That fireball wasn't your imagination. All three of us saw that,' Marc said thoughtfully. 'I have to go back to the library now to see if I can dig up any more info on Uriel.'

'I know someone who might know more about Uriel than all your computer records,' Colette said. She pointed to the spire of Saint Michael's church in the distance. 'Father Kimber would know all about ghosts and things like that.'

'That's not such a bad idea, Colette,' Marc said, and then remembered that he had left the PC still running up in the library. 'Wait here for me, and I'll meet you in ten minutes, OK?'

'You want to go and see him right away?'

'There's no time like the present, is there?' he said cheerfully.

After Marc had left for the library, Colette walked back over to the place where the fireball had been hovering. She knelt down and placed her hand over the scorch mark on the ground. She could still feel the heat – and that was crazy. Even she knew that, and she wasn't a scientist like Marc and Rebecca.

Suddenly she felt a prickling sensation in her palm. She sharply withdrew her hand. She stood up and turned it over.

Her palm was a deep pinkish colour. It reminded her of times when she'd accidentally plunged her hands into water that was much too hot for her. Only this time her palm felt not wet, but dry and itchy.

Colette . . . Colette . . .

Colette turned sharply around.

'Who is it?' she asked urgently. 'Who's there? Marc, is that you?'

Colette . . . Help me . . .

Colette's eyes darted this way and that but she could see no one. The yard was empty. Yet still the voice repeated her name. She raised her hand to her brow. She'd suddenly developed a raging headache, and she was running a temperature. Beads of sweat appeared on her forehead; she felt nauseous in the pit of her stomach. Her hand started to tingle.

Colette . . . Colette . . .

And now she was finding it difficult to breathe. Her lungs! It was as though they were burning!

Colette . . . Help me please . . . Only you . . .

'Who are you? Where are you? Why won't you go and leave me alone!'

The mysterious voice fell silent. Apart from the fact that the May afternoon now felt cold and creepy, it was as if nothing unusual had happened.

Colette shuddered. She glanced over to the main Institute building. Was it her imagination or was someone watching her from one of the top-floor windows?

Colette blinked. When she opened her eyes again the figure at the window had vanished, and Colette decided that it must have been her imagination.

But that voice hadn't been her imagination. She was sure of that. And what was more, it was the same voice that had been haunting her for the past few weeks now. It was a male voice, scared, frightened, and confused. A male voice which Colette recognised as being distinctly American.

*Dateline: Classroom M9, The Institute;
Wednesday 9th May; 15.50.*

'Dr Molloy, can I see you for a moment?' Rebecca asked, after she had knocked at the classroom door and entered.

Dr Molloy looked up from behind her desk where she was marking a set of exam papers, and smiled. Rebecca was one of her favourite pupils.

'Of course,' she said and put down her red pen. Rebecca approached her desk and resisted the temptation of glancing down at the marked exam papers. Instead she looked up at the whiteboard behind her teacher. *Concepts of Euclidean Geometry and its Modern-Day Application*, the words read. It seemed that today's lesson wasn't going to be exactly riveting.

'You must be keen,' Dr Molloy said with a smile and gathered the papers together before placing them in the desk drawer. 'Class isn't for another ten minutes.'

'Who is Joseph Williams?' Rebecca asked, coming straight to the point.

'Joseph Williams?' Dr Molloy's face fell. She looked nervously over Rebecca's shoulder. Through the open door she could see students and teachers walking off to their various lessons. 'How do you know about him?'

'Marc Price and I were looking through the school register,' Rebecca said. 'According to that, you're his personal tutor. Who is he? Why haven't either of us seen him here?'

Dr Molloy tore her eyes away from the open door and looked at Rebecca. 'Exactly why do you want to know?' she asked curiously.

Rebecca frowned. Was it her imagination or was there a frightened look in the schoolteacher's eyes? 'We're curious, that's all,' she said. 'The Institute's one of the most famous schools in the world. You don't just get a scholarship here and then decide not to turn up.'

Dr Molloy stood up and went over to close the classroom door. Then she returned to her desk.

'What else do you know about Joey?' she asked.

'Nothing. That's why I'm asking you.'

'I met him when I took that year off to do my research paper at Colombia University,' she told Rebecca.

'So he was one of your students in New York?'

'Not exactly. He tried to snatch my bag in the street.'

'So what has he got to do with the Institute?'

'I was going to report him to the authorities, but then I discovered that, for a boy his age, he was a mathematical genius. Perfect Institute material. I arranged a scholarship for him. Eva was very helpful in persuading the General to agree.'

'Eva helpful? She's only ever seems to be interested in herself.' Rebecca suddenly remembered she was talking to a teacher. 'Sorry. I was out of order there.'

Dr Molloy waved aside Rebecca's apology. In fact, Rebecca had the feeling that the maths teacher was finally relieved to be talking to someone about this mysterious boy.

'He was due to arrive in England at the beginning of April,' she continued. 'But his arrival was delayed because of his sister's funeral.'

'Funeral?'

'A hit-and-run in Harlem,' Dr Molloy explained. 'The poor boy almost had a nervous breakdown. It must have been hard for him – he'd lost his mother the year before.'

'I'm not surprised. I was really cut up when Dad died – Wait a minute, did you say a car accident?'

'That's right,' Dr Molloy said and frowned. 'Is there something wrong?'

'No, nothing at all,' Rebecca lied, remembering what Colette had said about her nightmares. She'd told them that she'd dreamt about a car accident, hadn't she?

'He boarded the plane at JFK airport, but never arrived in London. Or at least that's what they told me.'

'You don't believe them?'

'Rebecca, I saw Joey get off that plane.'

'Didn't you say anything to the police?'

'Of course. They passed me from department to department then finally told me that there wasn't a case to investigate. There'd been a glitch in the booking system at JFK and Joey had never got on the plane.'

'I suppose these things happen occasionally,' Rebecca said.

'And I suppose I might have been mistaken at Heathrow,' Dr Molloy said and looked meaningfully

at Rebecca. Each of them knew that Dr Molloy never
made mistakes.

'But why would he turn down a place at the
Institute? When I got my own scholarship, it was one
of the happiest days of my life.'

'We'll never know now,' Dr Molloy said. 'I tried to
ring his father.'

'And?'

'He died of an accidental overdose the day after
Joey left for London,' she finished.

'Kids do go missing all the time,' Rebecca said.
'Especially in New York.'

'Rebecca, I saw him get off the plane at Heathrow – '
Click!

Rebecca and Dr Molloy turned around sharply in
the direction of the noise. The classroom door, which
the maths teacher had closed, was now slightly ajar.

Rebecca marched over to the door, and pulled it
open. There was no one there. The corridor was empty.
It was quiet too, apart from the unmistakable *squeak-
squeak-squeaking* sound of a wheelchair being pushed
away. And there was the trace of a certain fragrance in
the air as well.

Rebecca and Dr Molloy exchanged anxious looks.
How long had they been there? How much had they
heard?

Rebecca was about to go off in the direction of the
wheelchair when the buzzer for the next period
sounded. The corridor suddenly filled with students
on their way to their next lessons.

As Rebecca's fellow students streamed into the

maths room, Dr Molloy drew closer to Rebecca and whispered into her ear so that only she would hear.

'What I've told you about Joey Williams, forget about it,' she said. 'That is, if you value your future here at the Institute . . .'

The Power in the Earth

Dateline: Saint Michael's Church;
Wednesday 9th May; 15.45.

Marc and Colette found Father Emmanuel Kimber in
the belltower of Saint Michael's Church. He was looking out over the surrounding countryside through a
small telescope on a metal mount. When Marc
coughed to announce their presence, he jumped with
fright, and spun around on his heels, almost knocking
over the telescope in the process.

'Goodness gracious me!' he spluttered as he saw
who it was.

Marc and Colette exchanged a smile. They hadn't
thought that anyone ever used words like that
anymore.

'Don't sneak up on an old man like that!' Kimber
said. His voice was thin and reedy and matched his

appearance. The new parish priest of Saint Michael's was a slightly built man, with a likeable face, a beaky nose, a yellowish complexion and a shock of white hair. There was a merry twinkle in his green eyes. Marc guessed that he must be somewhere in his early fifties.

'I'm sorry, sir.'

Kimber peered at Marc through the tiny pair of *pince-nez* spectacles which were perched precariously on the end of his hawkish nose.

'Eh, what's that?' He leant forward to hear Marc better. It seemed that the new priest was a trifle deaf.

'I said I'm sorry, sir,' Marc repeated. He couldn't resist a smile. There was something rather endearing about Father Emmanuel Kimber.

'And who might you be, young man?'

'This is Marc Price, Father,' Colette said. 'He studies at the Institute.'

Kimber looked at Marc with renewed interest. 'Does he now?' he said. 'With Miss Eva?'

'You know Eva?' Marc asked in surprise. The woman and the parish priest seemed as unalike as chalk and cheese: Eva so cold and calculating; Kimber, bumbling and amiable.

'Yes, she comes here quite often.'

'That doesn't sound like her at all,' Marc remarked. The idea of Eva on her knees, praying, was almost impossible to contemplate. He indicated the telescope, whose metal base was glinting in the afternoon sun. 'I see you're interested in astronomy, sir,' he said.

'Wrong time of day for it though, isn't it?' Colette said cheekily.

'Aha, but I wasn't looking at the stars, Miss Russell,' Kimber said, and invited her to look through the telescope. It was trained on the church steeple in the neighbouring village.

'Checking out the opposition then, are you, sir?' Marc grinned after he, too, had taken a look through the telescope.

'The very idea!' Kimber chuckled. 'Look a little to the left of the church and tell me what you see.'

Marc did as he was told. 'It's that ancient stone circle on the Darkfell Rise,' he said.

'That's right,' Kimber said. 'Centuries ago, pagans used to worship there. And what do you see beyond that?'

'Another church, and then another, and another,' Marc realised and looked up. 'They're all perfectly lined up with each other.'

'Exactly, Mr Price!' Father Kimber said. 'You'll find the same thing all over England, in Europe as well. Sacred sites and holy places. Churches. Ancient monuments. Sacred groves. Pyramids. Beacon hills where they lit the sacrificial fires. All standing in exact alignments to each other.'

'Ley-lines,' Marc said knowledgeably.

'What do you know about them?' Father Kimber said. He peered even closer at Marc.

'They're supposed to be built along lines of geomagnetic force, aren't they?' he said. 'Forming a natural energy grid throughout the whole countryside.'

'You mean, sort of like invisible power cables

running underneath the earth?' Colette asked, trying to put it into language she could understand.

'I wouldn't have thought that Institute students would be interested in such things.' Father Kimber said.

'Well, actually, it's sort of sacred sites that we wanted to talk to you about,' Marc said.

'Indeed?' Now Father Kimber was very interested. Yet despite this, he said, 'All this ley-line business is nonsense, of course. Sensible people say that they're nothing more than what's left of old salt-traders' routes from the Neolithic era.'

'Then why are you interested in them, Father?' Colette asked. 'If I didn't know any better I'd say that you were trying to put Marc off. And why should you do that?'

Father Kimber chuckled. 'Not at all, my dear girl,' he said. 'I just thought that there'd be enough to study at the Institute.'

'Maybe the Institute is on one of your ley-lines as well,' Colette said.

'Eh? How do you make that out?' Father Kimber wanted to know.

'Well, you do know that the Institute was built on the site of an old convent?'

'I imagine it was Henry VII who tore the old place down.'

'Sorry, sir?'

'What do they teach you at that Institute of yours? Henry VII and the Dissolution of the Monasteries. Horrible man.'

'The eighth, sir,' Marc corrected him. 'Henry VIII was responsible for the Dissolution of the Monasteries.'

'Of course.'

'And anyway, the convent was burnt down,' Marc continued enthusiastically as he warmed to his subject. 'Did you ever hear of the legend of Sister Uriel who's supposed to haunt the area on April 30th?'

'It's called Beltane,' Colette added helpfully. 'It's an ancient pagan festival.'

'So this ghost – this demon, is supposed to appear at Beltane?'

'Yes,' said Marc, who had never really thought of Sister Uriel as a demon before. He started to feel a little foolish. 'I guess it looks like she's been held up.'

'Or maybe she's just running to a different schedule from the rest of us,' Father Kimber said mysteriously.

'What do you mean?' asked Marc.

'Isn't it obvious?' Kimber asked, and, when Marc had told him that, no, it wasn't obvious, he continued: 'Back in the eighteenth century the calendar in England was altered by ten days to put it in line with the rest of Europe. So that would mean, that, say, April 30th became May 10th.'

'And that would mean that the real Beltane is in a few days' time!'

'Exactly!' Kimber said, and his voice took on a deeper, darker tone.

He leant forward so that his beaky nose was almost touching Marc's and gazed deeply into his eyes. 'Don't involve yourself with the forces of darkness, my boy, not at this time of the year. There are terrible creatures out there. Demons and forces we can't even begin to understand.'

Marc gulped. He was feeling uneasy.

'Please, Marc, stay away from her, do you hear?' Father Kimber was pleading now. 'Don't believe your teachers at the Institute, my boy, who might say that such things don't exist. They do.'

Even though the sun was shining on the belltower it now seemed very cold indeed. Marc glanced away from Father Kimber and saw a stone gargoyle staring malevolently back at him. He shuddered.

'Of course we will. Won't we, Colette?'

There was no reply. Marc realised that Colette hadn't said a word since she had told Kimber about Beltane. She had vanished.

'She must have gone back into the church,' he said, and started to move off towards the narrow spiral stairwell which led back down into the main body of the church.

'Goodbye, dear boy,' Kimber said. 'And please – don't forget what I said.'

'I won't, sir,' Marc said and headed back down the stairs.

He found Colette in the church nave, looking towards the altar stone. Her back was to him, and she jumped when he announced his presence.

'What are you doing down here?' he asked. She turned around to look at him, her face hidden in the shadows.

'I thought I heard someone calling my name,' she told him.

Marc looked around in the shadows. 'There's nobody here.'

'I know.'

Colette stepped forward and the light streaming in through the stained-glass window shone on her face. Marc gasped.

'What is it, Marc?' Colette asked, as he reached out a hand and lightly touched her left cheek.

'You've bruised yourself,' he said.

'How can I have done?' asked Colette. She took a mirror out of the back pocket of her jeans. Sure, enough, there was a blue-black swelling just below her left eye.

'I don't understand,' she said. 'I haven't hit myself or anything.'

'Maybe Father Kimber is right and we should stop investigating Uriel,' Marc said. 'He's just been warning me about her. Predicting all sorts of disasters if we carry on snooping around.'

'That's odd, his pooh-poohing your idea about ley-lines, and then saying that Uriel exists, isn't it?'

Marc and Colette turned as they heard Father Kimber enter the main part of the church. When he saw Colette's bruise he was immediately full of concern.

'My dear child, has someone hit you?' he asked.

'No,' she said and shook her head. 'It just seemed to appear from nowhere.'

Father Kimber looked intently at her. 'And has this sort of thing ever happened to you before?' he asked searchingly.

'No,' Colette said truthfully.

'You've never had any strange feelings?' he asked.

'Well, I – ' Colette started but Marc interrupted. He was really concerned about her.

'Father, don't you have some ointment or something?' he asked.

'Yes, of course,' Father Kimber said, although his mind seemed to be elsewhere. 'Follow me.'

He led Colette and Marc into a small anteroom where he proceeded to dab at the bruise from a small bottle of antiseptic which he kept on a bookshelf.

Marc glanced at some of the titles. *Operation Desert Storm*, by Alastair Courtenay, who he recalled had been one of Axford's comrades during the Gulf War. *Register of the British Army*, another book he'd seen on the General's shelves. *The Old Straight Track*, an old-fashioned looking book by someone called Alfred Watkins. *Thermonuclear Physics*, by E. C. Kesselwood. *Journal of the Paranormal and Unexplained* by Damaris Hawthorne. They weren't exactly the titles he'd expect to find in a priest's library. Several of them had yellow post-it notes sticking out of them, marking particular pages of interest.

'No,' Colette went on. 'It just appeared . . . from out of nowhere . . . '

'Could it be Uriel?' Marc asked awkwardly.

Father Kimber looked up. For a second it seemed that he didn't recognise the name, which was odd, as he had just been warning Marc about her.

'Who? Oh, your Sister Uriel. Yes, of course, that's who it must be.' He turned back to Colette. 'So this bruise just appeared from out of nowhere then, did it, my child?'

'Yes, that's what I said.'

'And once again, nothing like this has ever happened to you before? Nothing strange? Nothing inexplicable?'

Marc and Colette looked at each other, uncertain how much they should tell Father Kimber. Finally Marc made a decision.

'Sir, you believe in ghosts, don't you?'

'Of course, I do. I've told you that already. Stop investigating Uriel. She will only come to harm you.'

'But that's the point, sir. She already has,' Marc said. 'She burnt down the school kitchens.'

'That was merely an electrical fire,' Kimber said. 'That is what General Axford told me when I went over to visit him.'

'That's what he was told, yes,' Marc said.

'You know something else?' Kimber demanded.

Marc stared at the priest, unsure what to tell him. Would the priest believe him if Marc told him about the ball of fire in the yard?

'The Institute must be haunted,' Colette said, and Father Kimber's face became grim, when she told him about the legend of Uriel.

'So she's supposed to reappear every hundred years,' Kimber asked. 'And the abbey was burnt down in the 1700s. Did she reappear in the 1800s?'

Marc started to feel a little foolish. 'Well, no, not that I know of . . .' he admitted.

'There *was* a fire!' Colette said. 'I remember reading

it when my father bought the deeds to the land. Towards the end of the 1800s, when the Institute was still a country house, there was a massive fire in the stables – '

'And the kitchens were built on that site,' Marc realised.

Father Kimber looked darkly at each of them. 'So it may be true, then,' he said. 'Uriel has returned. Stay away from her, my children, stay away from her. Forget everything about her. Only the Lord or the Devil knows what might happen . . .'

Dateline: The Project;
Wednesday 9th May; 16.13.

Joey gritted his teeth as White Mask hit him once again across the face. Already there was a large swelling under his left eye. He'd have given anything now to kick out at the older man, but the leather straps still bound him tightly to the bench.

The thing Joey wanted to do most in the world was scream, but he willed himself not to. To show any pain would be to let that limey streak of ditchwater know that he was winning. And if there was one thing that Joey hated most, it was letting anybody over the age of thirty get one over on him.

'And what was that for, dog-breath?'

'For disobeying my orders,' White Mask said. He looked at the bank of computers on the far wall. 'The screens over there monitor your brainwave patterns. They show an unusually high level of activity.'

'So?'

'Your talents are to be used only when – and how – I instruct you to do so.'

'Take a hike, granddad,' Joey replied, even though he wasn't quite sure what he'd done. One minute he was lying strapped to the bench and then it was as if he'd gone asleep and was talking to this young kid in a church somewhere. But who she was he hadn't the faintest idea.

'You were trying to communicate with someone – who was it?' White Mask demanded.

'I don't know what you mean,' Joey said truthfully. He remembered Sara and how they'd often known what each other was thinking. Was this something similar? But who was this strange girl? And why was her face so familiar?

'Do so again, and Omar here will ensure that your throat is cut from side to side.'

He called over the Middle Eastern man who had picked Joey up at the airport all those days ago. There was a gleam in his dark and cruel eyes which suggested that he'd rather enjoy carrying out White Mask's threat.

Omar stalked menacingly towards Joey. He struggled in his leather bonds, which refused to budge but just cut deeper into his skin. White Mask and Omar smiled when they saw the look of panic in his eyes.

Suddenly a telephone rang. White Mask left Joey's side and took the mobile from out of the pocket of his white lab coat. He cupped his mouth over the receiver, so that Joey couldn't hear what he was saying. After he'd hung up, he called Omar over, exchanged a few words with him, and then they both left the room.

Joey lay on the bench for what seemed like hours before the door clicked open again and he heard the sound of familiar footsteps *click-click-clacking* across the floor towards him.

'Joey, what have they done to you?' Maria asked, when she saw the bruise under his left eye.

'What does it look like?'

'They shouldn't have hurt you . . .'

'Try telling White Mask that. Or that creep, Omar. He doesn't say much does he? Doesn't speak English well, I suppose?'

'The Project is International,' Maria said. 'And believe me, Joey, we don't mean to hurt anyone.'

'You could have fooled me,' Joey snarled. 'And what about these other kids I've heard dog-breath talk about? Did you "not hurt" them, as well?'

Maria shuddered. 'That was unfortunate,' she said.

'Unfortunate? Unfortunate for who?' Joey demanded, and then he softened his tone. So far Maria had been the only one to show any kind of sympathy towards him. He couldn't afford to make an enemy out of her. 'Where've White Mask and his thug gone to?'

'The Project's Deputy Controller has arrived. They're in conference at the moment.'

'So White Mask isn't the head honcho of this set-up then?'

'Of course not. He's just one of many people all over the world who work for the Project.'

'But what does this Project of yours do? And what is the Mindfire?'

'Hush. The Professor – I mean, White Mask – has forbidden me to tell you,' Maria said, 'but believe me, it's for the good of everyone.' She started checking the meters and read-outs on the computer bank, and adjusted a few switches on the helmet attached to Joey's head.

Joey looked slyly at the nurse. 'Maria, I'm hurting,' he told her.

'It'll pass.' She checked one of the brainwave monitoring screens above Joey's head. 'You shouldn't have tried to try to use your powers so soon after creating a Mindfire. The brain needs time to recover from all that psychic stress.'

'It's not just my head,' Joey said slyly. 'It's these straps as well.'

'They'll be unfastened when it's time for you to go to bed.'

'I can't wait,' Joey said sarcastically. His bedroom, if you could call it that, was a windowless stone cell with a bunk bed, and a guard on constant duty outside the locked door. Even back home in Harlem things hadn't been that bad.

Maria checked the leather thongs that fastened Joey's arms and legs down to the bench.

'Please loosen them a little for me, Maria.'

Maria was uncertain for a moment, and then smiled. 'I don't see what harm it can do,' she said. She bent over and adjusted the straps. 'Now, is that better?'

Joey said it was, and Maria turned to go. 'And believe me, your headaches will go,' she promised him.

'They'd better,' Joey said. 'I haven't had one like this since they started real bad when my sister was killed by that hit-and-run driver.'

'Your sister was *killed*?'

'Yeah, by some prize maniac the cops never found,' Joey told her bitterly. 'No number plate, no nothing. But if I ever find who did it I swear I'll kill him – Hey, Maria, is there anything wrong?'

'No, Joey,' Maria lied. 'There's nothing wrong at all . . .'

THE PSYCHIC ZONE

8

Escape

Dateline: The Project;
Wednesday 9th May; 20.20.

It was dark now in the Project. No one had visited Joey for several hours now except for Maria, who had made her regular check on his temperature and heart-beat before returning to her business in some other part of the underground base.

Joey knew from experience that White Mask would return in about an hour's time, to take him back to his cell for the night. If he was to make his escape then this was the time to do it.

He twisted and turned on the bench, trying to slip his arms out of the leather straps which Maria had loosened. It was a hard struggle, but eventually he managed to wrench them free, scraping the skin on his wrists as he did so.

Joey gave a silent whoop of triumph, and then flicked a few buttons on the helmet as he'd seen White Mask do so many times before. Then he lifted the machine off his head.

There was a tiny bleep from one of the overhead monitors to which the helmet was attached. Joey froze for several minutes, but no one came into the chamber. He sat up on the bench and reached down to unfasten the straps around his ankles. If he was quick he would be able to escape before anyone even noticed he was missing.

Suddenly he heard footsteps coming from the corridor outside. Hurriedly he lay back down on the bench, replaced the helmet on his head, and lay the straps around his wrists and ankles to give the impression that he was still secured to the bench.

The door to the chamber creaked open. Joey was expecting White Mask to enter the room, but instead it was Omar who came through the door, and crossed over to him. Joey stared up defiantly at the stylishly-dressed thug.

'Where's White Mask tonight?'

'With the Deputy Controller.'

'And who's he?'

'You'll find out soon enough. They want to see you now.'

Omar reached over for Joey's helmet. Fortunately for Joey, Omar was no scientist, so he didn't notice that the device had already been disconnected. Omar set the helmet on one side and then walked to the foot of the bench.

As he bent down to unfasten the leather straps around Joey's feet, Joey saw his chance and kicked him savagely in the face. Omar howled with pain and fell back, spluttering a curse in Arabic.

Joey rolled off the bench, and headed for the open door. But Omar was too quick for him, even with blood streaming from his nose. He grabbed hold of Joey with both arms, crushing him in a vice-like grip.

But Joey's fists were free, and he fought back, thumping the man in the stomach. For a moment Omar's hold on Joey weakened. A moment was all that Joey needed. He squirmed out of Omar's grip, stamped down hard on his feet, and then ran to the open door, slamming it shut in Omar's face.

Joey gave himself just a half-second to look in both directions down the empty passageway. He knew that one way led back to his cell and a dead end, so there was no choice but to take the other route. Omar had already thrust open the door and was following him.

Against one wall of the passageway someone had lined up several wooden boxes. As he raced past them, Joey flung them into Omar's path. Omar cursed, lost his balance, and went crashing to the floor.

Joey turned a corner. The passage now forked off in three directions. He glanced back nervously. Omar would be coming round the corner any moment now. There was no time to lose. He had to choose which way to go and he had to choose it now.

He took the left-hand fork just as he heard Omar pick himself up off the ground. Omar's footsteps came closer. Joey started to run, and then heard two other sets of footsteps come echoing down the corridor from the other direction. He hid behind one of the packing cases, just before Omar met the two newcomers at the junction of the three forks.

'What's happened?' It was White Mask's voice.

'The Williams brat has escaped,' Omar said. 'Someone must have freed him.'

'Maria,' White Mask guessed.

'I told you she was too soft-hearted to work for the Project,' said Omar.

Then Joey's blood chilled as he heard the voice of the Deputy Controller of the Project. It was husky and cold and full of evil.

'Find the child. Capture him alive if you can. We still have uses for his psychic talents. But kill him if necessary. And, gentlemen – '

'Yes?' asked White Mask and Omar.

'Fail and I shall take the greatest pleasure in squeezing the last drop of life out of both of you myself.'

Joey heaved a sigh of relief as he heard the three of them walk off in the opposite direction. When he was sure that they had gone, he came out of his hiding place, and looked around.

The passage he had taken seemed to finish in a dead-end. However, a few metres further down the tunnel, several stone steps had been built into the wall. Joey frowned. What was the point of steps going nowhere? He climbed the first step and looked up.

There was a large rectangular slab set into the ceiling. It reminded Joey of the trap door which led into his old aunt's attic back in New York State. Perhaps this was a way out of the Project's underground tunnels?

Joey climbed on to the second stone step, and reached up to touch the trap door. Nothing happened. He looked around for some sort of opening mechanism. There was none to be seen.

Perhaps if he looked a little closer? He climbed on to the third step. And then the fourth one.

As soon as he set his foot on the final step, he felt it sink a little beneath him. Then he heard the sound of a hidden mechanism, and the stone slab above his head slid away.

Joey reached and pulled himself up through the opening in the ceiling. At last he was going to be free! He heaved himself through the exit.

He carefully slid the stone slab back to cover his escape route. It seemed to be mounted on castors so that, despite its apparent weight, it moved easily. He looked around. Apart from a small chink of light about three metres from him, the room he was in was dark. And its stone walls were cold and damp – as cold and damp as a grave. Not that it bothered Joey particularly. All he was concerned about was getting as far away from the Project – and as quickly as possible.

He heard a skittering noise from the far corner of the room, and he froze. He peered into the darkness, but he could see nothing.

'Who's there?'

There was no reply, just the squeaking of a rat or a mouse, as it hid itself away from Joey, more scared of him than he was of it.

Joey's eyes quickly adjusted themselves to the darkness. He saw that the room was bare, apart from what looked like a large stone table in the corner. On the table someone had spread out a map, several pencils and a pair of old-fashioned protractors and a set square. On the stone floor beside the desk was piled another set of maps.

Unable to resist his own curiosity, Joey picked up and squinted at the open map, holding it towards the chink of light so that he could see it more clearly.

It was an Ordnance Survey of Brentmouth village and the surrounding area. Several points on the map had been ringed in red ink. Saint Michael's Church. The ring of stones on the Darkfell Rise. Saint Wulfrida's in nearby Fetchwood. The Institute itself. A couple of prominent hills to the north-west. Someone had drawn lines between each and every one of these points.

It was obvious that it all meant something, but Joey had no time to stop and wonder – White Mask and Omar would soon have worked out where he had gone and would be coming after him. He headed towards the chink of light, which was coming from a half-open door.

As Joey did so he noticed the pile of maps on the floor. Curiosity got the better of him and he paused to take a look. Cairo and Surrounding Districts. Ayers Rock in Australia. Kuwait. Salisbury Plain, which he guessed was somewhere in England. What did they all have in common with each other? he wondered.

Joey cursed himself. There was no time to waste. He

should be making good his escape and not pondering over old maps. He pushed open the heavy door, and found himself stumbling out into the chill night air.

Joey felt grass beneath his feet and saw the stars in the sky overhead. He glanced behind him. The building he had just come out of looked like a tiny stone outhouse. Maybe years ago, local farmers had used it to store their produce.

About a mile away, he could just make out the lights of the Institute. Or at least he guessed that it was the Institute. He thought he recognised it from photographs he'd seen, even in the fading light. Dr Molloy would be there, he realised. She could help him. Heck, no one else could.

He was about to run off in the direction of the school buildings when a thought struck him. It was Dr Molloy who had arranged for him to attend the Institute in the first place. Who was to say that she hadn't been responsible for having him kidnapped and brought to the Project's underground base?

But maybe there was just one person he could still trust, Joey thought. He remembered the girl in his head. *Young white girl about his age. Short, blonde hair. Impish face. Kinda pretty*. He looked to the south and saw lights blazing in the faraway windows of a big house on the other side of the Darkfell Rise. And though he didn't know the name of the person who lived there, although he had only ever seen her face in a newspaper on the day his sister had died and his headaches had started to hurt more than they had ever done before, Joey started to run towards Colette

Russell's house. In a way, he had no choice. He was like iron being drawn to a magnet. Or a fly being dragged into a spider's web.

So intent was Joey on his escape that he didn't see the door to the stone outbuilding open once again. Nor did he see the three figures who stepped out into the moonlight. Omar reached inside his jacket, pulled out a revolver and aimed it at Joey's departing figure. The Deputy Controller, however, stayed his hand.

'No.'

'I thought you said you wanted him killed.' Omar's face fell. He'd hadn't killed anyone in quite a while and he was rather looking forward to it.

'But not yet, not here. The Project has survived for fifty-one years by learning how to be discreet, Omar. Follow him. Find out where he is going.

'And what shall we do about Maria?' White Mask asked the Deputy Controller after Omar had vanished off into the night.

The Deputy Controller gave him an icy smile. 'I will leave that to your own discretion, Professor. The Williams child still has value for us. The nurse has outserved her usefulness. Make sure that no one will ever find the body.'

'Very well, Deputy Controller,' White Mask said and returned inside the stone outbuilding, leaving the Deputy Controller standing alone in the moonlight.

The Deputy Controller of the Project stared up at the full moon for a few moments and then started walking off in the opposite direction to Joey and Omar. The Deputy Controller had many other things to attend to at the Institute. And Joey Williams and the Mindfire were only one.

Dateline: Fiveways;
Wednesday 9th May; 23.11.

'Who's there?' Colette asked nervously. She was standing at the bottom of the stairs of Fiveways, her parents' house, and looking at the kitchen door. Behind the door's frosted glass, she could make out a dark shape, knocking to be let in.

'Colette! Colette!'

Colette shuddered. It was that voice again, the same voice she'd been hearing in her head for weeks now, and the same voice that she'd heard in Saint Michael's church. Was she dreaming it? She hoped she was. It was much preferable to the other alternative: that she was going mad.

'Colette! Colette!'

'Go away!' Colette cried. 'You're nothing to do with me! You're part of my imagination!'

She looked back up the stairs, wondering whether she should just go back to bed and lock the bedroom door. She'd heard the voice in her sleep and, when she'd woken up, she'd thought that it had been her mother calling out to her. Then she'd remembered that tonight was when her mother went out to one of her local charity meetings and that she wouldn't be back until late.

So then she had thought that it was Miss Kerr, the housekeeper. But Colette recalled seeing Miss Kerr sneak out to the local pub after she'd gone to bed, so it couldn't be her either.

'Colette! Colette! Open up!'

Colette had always been taught never to open the door to strangers. But this stranger sounded so frightened. And it wasn't as though he really was a stranger, was it? Could you call anyone a stranger when you'd been hearing their voice in your head?

Finally, she went to the door and twisted the key in the lock. The door flew open and Joey came tumbling into the kitchen.

'Quick! Shut the door!'

'Why?' Colette asked. 'I don't understand.' She shut the door though.

'White Mask, that's why,' the boy said irritably, and then looked at Colette as though recognising her for the first time. 'You're Colette, aren't you?'

'Of course I am,' she said. 'But how do you know?'

'I've dreamt about you,' he said, 'ever since Sara . . .'

'But I've never seen you before in my life.'

'I know.'

He examined Colette's face much more closely. He remembered how he'd collapsed in the street when he'd discovered that Sara was dead. He remembered how the last thing he'd seen had been that photograph in the newspaper of some businessman big-wig and his pretty young daughter attending a function somewhere in New York.

Joey's stare made Colette feel distinctly uneasy, so she returned the stare and looked at the boy's own face.

'You've got a bruise below your left eye.'

'That's right,' he said, remembering when White Mask had struck him.

'So have I.'

'I don't see nothing,' Joey said.

'I used Mum's make-up to cover it,' she said.

'Your dad hit you?'

'Of course not,' Colette was outraged at the very suggestion. 'It just appeared this afternoon.'

'About the time I got hit,' Joey realised.

'Look, how do you know my name? Who are you? Who are you running away from?'

'They trapped me underground,' Joey said. 'They strapped me down to some weird kind of machine. It's what they call the Mindfire.'

Colette felt her heart skip a beat. 'Fire?'

'Yeah,' Joey said, and glanced back once more at the closed door. 'I don't really understand it, but somehow my mind can unlock some kinda elemental force. They tried it back in the Middle East – so Maria told me.'

'Daddy made his fortune with CompuDisk designing security equipment,' she told Joey, and led him into the livingroom.

'Look, this really isn't the time to chat about your old man's job – ' Joey began, but Colette silenced him with a look.

'A few months ago he was called to Kuwait, to look

into the security around some of the oil wells there,' she told him. 'They'd been going up in flames for no reason at all, and the oil barons suspected terrorists were behind it.'

'It was probably these other kids White Mask had captured,' Joey guessed. 'Those other kids who died.'

'We have to tell the police,' Colette decided.

'No!' Joey was adamant. 'Those guys picked me up at the airport with official passes. Believe me, they've got influence everywhere.'

'But we have to tell someone.'

'In the morning, OK? Can I stay here tonight?'

'You can stay in the spare room. You'll be safe there.'

There was a sudden noise in the driveway outside and both of them froze. Colette went to the window and drew back the curtain. Someone was coming up the drive. For a second, she thought it was one of the villains Joey had told her about. Then she breathed a sigh of relief.

'It's OK, it's only my mum on her way back home. You'd better get upstairs into the spare room before she sees you here.'

As Joey ran up the stairs, Colette didn't notice the other person, hiding behind a tree in the driveway. Omar cursed to himself as he saw Mrs Russell open the front door and walk into the house. Two children he could deal with, but an adult would pose more problems. He would have to keep watch and wait for the right moment to strike.

THE PSYCHIC ZONE

9

Firestorm

*Dateline: The Institute, Chemistry Lab 2B;
Thursday 10th May; 08.22.*

Marc was one of the first to arrive at the Institute that day, taking the five minute walk from the boys' hostel at the north-eastern end of the school grounds to the chemistry labs. In the pocket of his leather jacket he was carrying the lump of tungsten he'd found in the yard. The cross embedded in its centre felt smooth and cold.

The school building and the labs had been unlocked half an hour before, and the advanced security and alarm system surrounding the main Institute buildings and labs shut down. The security system had been one of Eva's ideas, Marc recalled.

He entered the spacious lab and was surprised to see that it wasn't empty. Eva was sitting at a desk in the far corner, working at one of the PCs. She looked up when he entered and watched him through her dark glasses as he walked over to the spectroscope machine at the far end of the lab. Then she returned to her work, but over the next half-hour or so Marc was constantly aware of her presence.

As he started about his work, the door opened and Rebecca entered. She cast a wary look at Eva before crossing over to Marc.

'What's she doing here?' she asked.

'She said that her computer in Axford's office had crashed and she wanted to use one in the labs,' he told her.

'And do you believe her?'

'No. What are you doing here so early?'

'I was going to ask the same question of you,' she said. 'I called round at the boys' hostel and they told me you'd come here. What are you doing?'

Marc looked behind him to check that Eva wasn't listening. 'Doing a spectroscopic analysis of that tungsten, to see if there's any iron in it.'

'And if there isn't?'

'Then all the known laws of physics have just been broken,' he said cheerfully.

'They already have been,' Rebecca reminded him. 'And there's something else too: I was talking to Dr Molloy about Joey Will – '

'Good morning, Miss Storm. Good morning, Mr Price.'

Rebecca and Marc turned around. Once again Eva had crept silently up on them. In her hand she was holding a floppy disk and a computer print-out. She looked curiously at Marc's experiment. 'And what is this?'

'Just a little project of ours, Eva,' Marc said hurriedly.

'I'm pleased that you start work so early,' Eva said approvingly, 'but I think it is time for your physics lesson now.'

Rebecca glanced at her watch. As usual Eva was right. Her physics class was due to begin in five minutes' time.

'How do you know my schedule so well?'

'I make it my business to know everything that goes on here at the Institute,' she informed her. 'I'm interested in everything you do.' She walked smartly out of the room.

Rebecca considered sticking her tongue out at Eva's departing figure, decided it was a highly immature thing to do, and then did it anyway.

'That's put you in your place, Bec!'

'Eva knows too much, more even than General Axford, I bet,' Rebecca said. 'There doesn't seem to be a thing that you can do without her being aware of it! Sometimes I wouldn't be surprised if she isn't – ' She stopped, realising how stupid she must sound.

'Isn't what?'

'Sometimes I get the feeling that she isn't really human.'

Dateline: Fiveways; Thursday 10th May; 08.30.

'Joey, are you awake?'

Colette tapped gently on the closed door of the guest bedroom. Slowly the door creaked open, and Joey stuck his head out of the room. He looked tired. He hadn't slept well the previous night. In his dreams he kept seeing White Mask peering over him, and Sara being mowed down mercilessly by that limo.

'Is the coast clear?'

'My mother's gone off to see some friends, Miss Kerr is down in the village, and my tutor's not due for another hour or so.'

'I have to get away from here. White Mask and Omar will be out looking for me.'

'Where will you go to? Do you have any money?'

'Omar and his thugs took my luggage from me when they nabbed me at Heathrow.'

'We can go to the Institute,' Colette said. 'Marc and Rebecca will know what to do.'

'Who are they?'

'Friends of mine. Scientist types. Maybe they'll know what that machine White Mask used on you is for. At least it'll take our minds off ghostly nuns and fireballs.'

'What did you say?'

'Fireballs.'

'The Mindfire.'

Joey hadn't told Colette exactly what had happened to him in the Project's secret underground base, and he was about to explain further when there was a knock at the front door.

'It's OK,' Colette said, and checked her watch. 'It'll only be my tutor.'

'You said he wasn't due for another hour.'

'So he's early,' Colette said. She started to move downstairs to answer the door. 'Relax, Joey, no one would try and attack you in broad daylight.'

'Maybe you're right.'

Colette had barely unlocked the front door when it was flung open, and she was knocked to the ground. Omar burst into the hallway, holding a loaded gun. He reached down and pulled Colette roughly to her feet. Colette struggled but Omar's grip on her arm was far too strong and his fingers dug deep into her flesh.

'The boy. Where is he!' Omar demanded.

'I don't know who you mean.'

'I followed him here last night,' Omar snarled. 'Now where is the Williams brat?'

'He's gone,' Colette lied. She cast a nervous glance up the stairs where Joey was hiding on the landing.

It was a fatal mistake. Omar threw Colette to the ground, and she smashed her head against the hall side-table. A thin line of blood trickled down her temple. Not caring whether she was hurt or not, Omar raced up the stairs, two steps at a time.

Joey turned and ran. If he could just reach the bedroom then he might be able to barricade himself in there, or perhaps even escape through an upstairs window.

'Run, Joey, run!' Colette screamed, even though her head was aching from the wound and she was finding it hard to remain conscious.

Omar reached out and grabbed Joey by the foot. Joey kicked out, and managed to shake Omar off. With all his limbs aching Joey headed for the bedroom door.

Then there was a deafening sound, and Joey crashed to the floor, face-down. From her position lying on the hall floor, Colette looked up to see Omar return his smoking gun to the holster beneath his jacket. Then he picked up Joey's motionless form, and walked slowly downstairs, past Colette and out into the driveway.

'You've killed him!' Colette said. 'You've gone and killed Joey!'

'No,' Omar said, without looking back. 'But when we've finished with him he's going to wish that he were dead.'

Dateline: The Institute, Chemistry Lab 2B;
Thursday 10th May; 10.45.

Marc wiped the sweat from off his brow, and then checked the read-out from the spectrograph. The read-outs comprised long strips of light-sensitive paper patterned with vertical bands of colour. By examining the colour and width of the bands he could determine the chemical composition of any substance.

There was no doubt about it, he thought. All the

tests had proved that there wasn't the slightest trace of iron ore in the tungsten they'd found in the yard. So what could have caused the magnetic deflection that he, Rebecca and Colette had witnessed?

He looked out of the lab window. Sunlight glinted off the lightning conductor on the top of Saint Michael's in the distance. He thought about those special ley-lines which some said criss-crossed the country like a gigantic power network. Like underground power cables, Colette had described them. Father Kimber had said they were nonsense even though he seemed to know quite a bit about them. Maybe he ought to pay the parish priest another visit.

Marc ran his fingers through his blonde hair in exasperation. 'Oh, Sister Uriel, why can't you be behind all this?' he said. 'Then all we'd have to do is perform a simple exorcism and all our problems would be solved!'

'Excuse me?' Antonio Degrossi, one of his fellow chemistry students and the only other person in the lab, was looking curiously at him.

'Sorry, Tony, you caught me talking to myself.'

'Looks like the heat's getting to you as well.' Antonio loosened the collar of his shirt. 'It is getting hotter, isn't it.'

'I thought it was my imagination,' Marc said, and looked out of the window once again. Outside the sky seemed dull and overcast; inside the lab it was hotter than a July day.

'Looks like the central heating's on the blink again,' Antonio said. 'You want a Diet Coke?'

'In the middle of class?'

'Why not?' Antonio asked. Their teacher had left them to their own devices and had gone off to the staff room to catch up on some marking.

'And what if Eva catches you sneaking off class for a crafty Coke? You know how she seems to be everywhere.'

Antonio shook his head. 'I saw her leave the Institute about an hour ago,' he told Marc. 'Otherwise do you think I'd dare?'

'In that case I'd love a Coke,' Marc said. Antonio left the lab for the vending machine in the junior commonroom.

Beads of sweat dropped from Marc's brow on to the paper on which he was making notes. He looked over at the thermometer on the wall. It read thirty-three degrees.

And rising.

Dateline: The Project; Thursday 10th May; 10.46.

'He isn't hurt then?' the Deputy Controller of the Project asked, as White Mask adjusted a control on Joey's helmet. Joey's right arm was in a sling.

'No. It's merely a flesh wound. He'll be coming round any second now.'

'Then I shall leave. The fewer people who see my face the better. And one more thing – '

'Yes?'

'I have made many allowances for you, Professor. I agreed for your base to be located in this particular underground chamber because that is what you wanted.'

'It is ideally located for the sort of work we want to carry out,' White Mask remarked.

'There are other places,' the Deputy Controller said. 'And not just here in Brentmouth village, as you well know. Stonehenge and Avebury. Cairo, and the Middle East on the lines connecting the Pyramids with Babylon, where you first came to my attention. Sacred sites, where the lines of geomagnetic force are so strong that a talented individual like the Williams brat can tap into that power, and use it as we see fit.'

'But there is no one else but me who has the technology to harness and channel the boy's psychic powers into the Mindfire,' White Mask pointed out.

'That is true,' the Deputy Controller admitted a little begrudgingly. 'Play your little game if you want, Professor, have your revenge. But remember one thing: nothing must harm the Institute! At least, not until I say so.'

And, with that, the Deputy Controller of the Project marched smartly away to attend to other business.

White Mask chuckled to himself and looked back down at Joey, who was just regaining consciousness. He smiled cruelly at him.

'Never try to escape from the Project again,' he stated coldly. 'The next time you won't be so lucky and Omar's bullet will find your heart.'

'My head hurts. Where's Maria?'

'Dead.'

'Maria, dead?'

'She allowed herself to be deceived by you. Therefore she had to die. There was no alternative.'

Joey shook his head from side to side. Maria was the only person to have shown him any sort of kindness down here at the Project. And now he had as good as gone and killed her. Just as he had as good as killed Sara when he'd refused to cross the road for those two Doctor Peppers.

Joey's brain felt as though it was going to explode as White Mask made some final adjustments to the computer banks behind him. A familiar pain stabbed into Joey's mind, and he heard that awful sound once again, the sound of the Mindfire.

Kreeee . . .

And he couldn't control it.

Dateline: The Institute, Chemistry Lab 2B;
Thursday 10th May; 10.47.

'Tone? Is that you?' Marc asked as the lab door opened behind him.

'Marc! You have to help!'

'Colette, what are you doing here?' Marc asked and stood up. He swayed a little: he was feeling a little giddy. Maybe it was this heat. When was Antonio going to arrive with that Coke?'

'I ran here as fast as I could,' she said. 'They've taken Joey!'

'Joey who?' Marc asked and then remembered. 'You mean Joseph Williams, the missing maths kid? Where have they taken him to? Who have taken him?'

But Colette was no longer listening. She pointed over Marc's shoulder to a pile of papers which had been left on the teacher's desk. They were beginning to crackle and brown around the edges.

Kreeee . . .

They both watched on in horror as a small pinprick of light appeared in the middle of the lab. It shuddered in mid-air, and started to grow, spitting out tongues of flame.

'Colette, let's get out of here . . .' Marc said and took her arm.

The ball of fire had already quadrupled in size in the space of a couple of seconds. Tongues of fire shot out all around them, cutting off their escape. The computer at the far end of the room shorted and blew. The overhead lights flickered and went out.

Already the curtains had caught fire. The flames spread towards the door. Marc and Colette heard a series of small explosions behind them. Several jars of inflammable chemicals shattered and burst.

Thick, noxious smoke filled the lab, and Marc and Colette could hardly see in front of them.

They weren't going to get out in time.

*Dateline: The Institute, Physics Lab 1A;
Thursday 10th May; 10.47.*

Rebecca yawned as she passed an electromagnetic charge through the coil of wire and glanced down at a meter to check the current being generated. It was a common enough experiment, and she had been frustrated when her physics teacher had asked her and her fellow students to perform it.

She frowned and then double-checked the readings. No doubt about it, the level of current being registered was only half of what she'd generated. Where had the rest of the electromagnetic force disappeared to?

She looked over to the far end of the room at the teacher's desk. Mr Boyle was busy marking exam papers and was too occupied to even notice her concern.

Simon Urmston came up to her. There was a worried expression on his face.

'What's up, Simon?'

Simon drew her attention to the transponder at the far end of the lab.

'It's just started playing up. The power isn't going through the induction coil like it should.'

'You've mis-set the controls?' Rebecca asked. Simon was a nice enough guy but he wasn't exactly the most precise of individuals.

'Of course not,' Simon said. He seemed quite affronted by the very suggestion. 'And what do you make of this?' He handed Rebecca a tiny compass, the sort she could buy in any high-street store. She looked at the compass and then gasped.

The compass needle was no longer pointing to the magnetic north. It was spinning madly out of control, changing from north to south, from east to west.

'This can't be happening!' she said, unwilling to believe the evidence of her own eyes. She wiped several beads of sweat from her brow: it was getting warmer.

'Maybe so, but it's still happening,' Simon reminded her. 'And the read-outs on the other meters are going wild too. It's just as if . . .'

Simon paused, unwilling to say what was on his mind.

'Just as if what?' Rebecca demanded.

'Just as if something's upsetting the Earth's geomagnetic field.'

'That's impossible!' Rebecca asserted. She was about to give Simon a whole series of reasons why nothing – well, nothing *natural*, anyway – could interfere with the lines of force running deep beneath the earth, when she froze.

Kreeee . . . kreeee . . . kreeee . . .

It was that dreaded sound again, the sound of evil to come. Her fellow students looked warily at each other. What was happening? Even Boyle glanced up from his marking.

The lab's overhead lights were starting to flicker. Suddenly they went out with a *whomp!*

Books started to topple off the shelves lining the lab wall. Test-tubes rattled menacingly in their racks.

A transponder started to crackle and then spark dangerously. Simon walked over and switched it off.

Instinctively Rebecca looked out through the open window, across the yard and towards the chemistry lab. Was Marc all right?

She watched in horror as the lab window was suddenly enveloped in a white and orange flame. The window exploded outwards in a shower of glass. Tongues of orange fire licked out of the room.

'Marc!'

In spite of what she saw, Rebecca kept her head. She told Simon to dial 999, and then raced out of the laboratory.

She covered the yard in less than half a minute, just as clouds of foul-smelling smoke were starting to billow up out of the shattered lab window on the first floor. Students were rushing out of the adjacent buildings, to see what was happening. From far off she could hear the whine of an approaching fire engine.

Rebecca pushed open the doors to the chemistry block and ran up the stairs. By the time she reached the landing, the area was full of smoke. She could hardly see her hand in front of her. The fumes stabbed into her lungs. She pulled a handkerchief out of her jeans pocket, placed it over her mouth, and headed for the closed lab door.

One thought nagged at her mind. *Why wasn't the automatic fire alarm sounding?* By rights it should have switched itself on as soon as the fumes reached the electronic smoke alarm, and activated the sprinkler system. This fire was exactly like the one which had destroyed the kitchens only a few nights ago. Had the fire alarm been affected by the strange power fluctuation they'd experienced in the other lab?

Rebecca pushed open the door, and a wave of intense heat hit her. It was almost a physical force and she staggered back. She started to cough, as she breathed in much more of the smoke than she'd intended to. The temperature was now almost too painful to bear.

Come on, Rebecca! she told herself, *think of icebergs!*

Steeling herself against the heat, and willing herself to ignore the searing pain in her lungs, Rebecca charged once more into the lab.

The place was ablaze, a hellish vision of fire and smoke. Several of the computers along the wall were shorting and adding their sparks to the inferno. Others had already started to melt. Jars of chemicals had exploded, spreading their acid contents over the floor.

Rebecca glanced up at the ceiling: the automatic sprinkler system remained defiantly switched off.

'Marc! Marc! Where are you?' she called out. She peered through the smoke which was starting to sting her eyes and make them water.

'Over here . . .' Marc croaked.

Rebecca looked down to the ground to see Marc on the floor. By his side Colette was almost unconscious. Rebecca raced over to him, and dragged first Marc, and then Colette, to their feet, and started to lead them to the door. They stumbled out on to the landing. Rebecca slammed the door shut behind them, in an attempt to halt the spread of the fire a little.

A waft of fresh air came up the stairs from the ground floor and brought Marc and Colette back to their senses. With Marc leaning on one shoulder and Colette on the other, Rebecca helped them down the steps and out towards the main exit.

Marc gasped in the precious, life-giving air, as the three of them stumbled outside.

'Marc, are you going to be OK?' Rebecca asked. Marc nodded, took a step away from her, and promptly collapsed to his knees. Rebecca bent down to help him up. To her relief she could hear the sound of approaching fire engines and ambulances.

'Uriel,' Marc spluttered.

'Don't be stupid – ' Rebecca began and then shut-up. Now wasn't the time to tell Marc to get real.

'It's true,' Colette said. 'We saw the ball of fire. She nearly killed both of us back there. Uriel doesn't want us to interfere. If we do then she'll destroy us all.'

THE PSYCHIC ZONE

10

A Hidden Persuader

Dateline: Brentmouth Cottage Hospital;
Thursday 10 May; 13.15.

Of course, Marc and Colette had to have medical treatment. The paramedics had insisted on that when they'd arrived on the scene. Oxygen masks had been strapped to their faces, and they'd been loaded aboard an ambulance for the cottage hospital.

Rebecca had gone along in the ambulance with them. They were grateful for her company. It had certainly been preferable to sharing the ride with Eva.

Eva had arrived back at the Institute just as the fire brigade were putting out the spluttering remains of the lab fire. For what was perhaps the first time ever, Eva's normal mask of icy composure cracked. She was seething with rage, and her fists clenched and unclenched. It was, as Marc cracked later in the hospital, not a pretty sight.

'It was Uriel,' Marc insisted to Rebecca as they waited in a small private room for the doctor to give him and Colette the all-clear to be discharged.

'Don't be ridiculous,' Rebecca said angrily. 'How can you possibly say that the ghost of a long-dead nun caused the accident in the lab?'

'It was the same ball of fire we saw in the yard,' Colette maintained.

'*And* it appeared when I was running checks on the cross in the tungsten,' Marc added. 'Perhaps Father Kimber was right after all and we should stay away from looking into Uriel too closely.'

At that moment the door opened and Father Kimber himself strode into the room. There was a concerned look on his face, as he walked over to Colette. 'My dear, dear child, are you all right?' he asked.

'I'm fine,' Colette said. Kimber turned to Marc.

'And you, my boy? Are you feeling well? Is there anything I can do for you?'

'I'm OK. But how did you know about the fire?'

'I was walking across the Rise to the Institute, when I saw the flames.'

'That's the second time you've been over to the Institute in the past couple of days,' Rebecca remarked.

'What do you mean?' Kimber asked.

'Remember?' Colette said. 'You gave me a lift there on the day we saw the ball of fire.'

'Colette!' Rebecca said. As far as she was concerned

this was still their secret and she didn't want anyone to know about the fireball, not even someone apparently so trustworthy as Father Kimber. She looked at the parish priest. He suddenly appeared very interested indeed.

'Ball of fire? What ball of fire?'

'The ball of fire that burnt down the labs,' Marc said.

'Miss Eva says the fire was down to some faulty wiring.'

'How could she know?' Marc said. 'We want to find out what's really going on.'

'What else do you know?' Father Kimber asked urgently.

'Nothing,' replied Rebecca. 'But we intend to find out more.'

Father Kimber looked darkly at Marc, and then at Colette, and Rebecca. Suddenly he no longer seemed the kindly, if slightly doddering, old parish priest they had known. 'So it's finally happening,' he said. 'Just as I knew it would.'

'What's finally happening?' Rebecca asked.

'The vengeance of Uriel.'

'Stop it!' Colette said. 'You're scaring me!'

'Good,' Kimber said.

'What do you mean?' asked Rebecca.

'If you're scared then perhaps you'll forget all about Uriel and stop dabbling with things you cannot control before you get hurt.'

'There's a mystery here and we intend to solve it,' Rebecca said firmly. 'You cannot put us off finding out the truth.'

'That's not what I'm concerned about,' Kimber claimed.

'Of course not,' Rebecca said, a little cynically.

'I'm concerned for your lives – your souls, if you like.'

'Sure.' Rebecca again. The way Kimber was talking, you'd've thought that they'd all stepped into some sort of melodrama.

'Please. For my own peace of mind, if not for your own. Forget about Uriel – before it's too late!'

Just then the door opened again and a nurse came in. Marc and Colette had another visitor, she told them.

'Eva? What's Eva doing here?' Marc wondered, after the nurse had revealed the identity of their visitor and had left the room to bring her in.

'You have another friend who wants to see you,' Father Kimber said hurriedly.

'Eva isn't a friend,' Rebecca said pointedly.

'I must go.'

'No, stay,' Marc said. 'I want to hear more about Uriel.'

Father Kimber was adamant, however. He left, but not before promising that he would pray for all their souls. Uriel was a force for evil, he warned them, and they would need all the help he could give them.

'It is nearly Beltane,' Marc said after he had left. 'Perhaps he's right and Uriel is out for her revenge.'

'Don't be stupid, Marc,' Rebecca said sternly. 'If I didn't know any better then I'd think that Kimber was trying to scare us off. What does he know about Uriel?

Why should he care about her? After all, he came to the village only a couple of weeks ago.'

'What has it to do with Joey?' Colette wondered.

'Joey?' Rebecca asked. In all the excitement neither Colette nor Marc had had the chance to tell Rebecca about Colette's late-night visitor.

'He's the one whose voice I keep on hearing in my head. He was kidnapped at the airport.'

'We have to go to the police,' Marc said.

'No, Joey doesn't want that.'

'Things are getting out of hand,' Rebecca said. 'This Joey Williams is kidnapped. The Institute has been put in danger by a ball of fire that defies all the known laws of physics. And you two very nearly get yourselves killed. We must tell General Axford.'

The door opened and the nurse escorted Eva inside. 'And what do you have to tell General Axford?' she asked them, as soon as the nurse had gone.

'Er, nothing,' Rebecca said.

'Then perhaps you can tell him nothing in person,' she said. 'I am to take you back to the Institute immediately.'

'You can't order me around like that,' said Colette. 'I'm not one of your students. My father owns the land the Institute's built on.'

'And he would be most distressed to hear that you had been entering the labs without permission, Miss Russell.'

'But –'

'Leave it, Colette,' Marc said. 'Do as she says.'

Eva smiled. 'I am glad that you are seeing sense at

last, Mr Price,' she said, and led the way out of the hospital.

Dateline: The Institute, General Axford's Office; Thursday 10th May: 14.43.

Marc, Rebecca and Colette followed Eva in silence to General Axford's office on the ground floor of the admin block. Eva opened the door. She didn't knock, but then that hardly surprised them. Ever since the General's accident Eva had been behaving as though she owned the place. She ushered them inside.

Axford was waiting for them behind his desk. The window behind him was open, and a chilly breeze was blowing through it which neither General Axford nor Eva seemed to notice. *But when you're as cold-hearted and emotionless as they are then why should they?* Marc thought.

The General stared at them through his alarming blue eyes, and then nodded to three chairs in front of his desk to indicate that they should sit down.

Eva went to her own considerably larger desk in the far corner of the room. The desk was cluttered with papers and files, as well as a row of phones. She pretended to start dealing with some paperwork, but kept an occasional wary eye on them.

'You are all right, Miss Russell, Mr Price, after your ordeal?' Axford asked.

Marc had the wildest idea that the man was actually concerned about their welfare.

'Yes, thank you,' Colette said. 'Marc was hurt more than me.'

'Sir, what happened?' he asked. 'Do we know how the fire started?'

'I was hoping you might answer that question, Mr Price. You were working in the lab, I believe. And you were alone there?'

'That's right. Until Colette came in.'

'Precisely what did occur in the library, Mr Price?'

Marc wondered how much he ought to tell Axford. He looked behind him. Eva was pretending to be working, but he knew that she was listening to every word he was saying.

'I was running a spectrograph check on a piece of tungsten,' Marc told him, 'when there was some kind of almighty explosion.'

'An explosion? One of the computers perhaps?'

Marc shook his head. 'It was far too big for that,' he said. 'There was an enormous bang and then everything caught fire.'

'And you have no idea what caused the explosion?'

'No, sir.'

Axford looked at Colette. 'And do you have any idea, Miss Russell?'

'I don't really understand all this scientific stuff,' Colette said. 'I came to see Marc and then – *bang!*'

Axford turned back to Marc. 'You wouldn't lie to me, would you?'

'No, sir,' Marc lied. He knew that Axford suspected he was hiding something from him. He looked over to Rebecca for help.

'Sir, there's something I think you should know,' Rebecca began. 'Just before the fire there was some kind of disturbance in the physics lab. All our instruments went crazy, just as if they'd been affected by an enormous magnetic field. Maybe that's why Eva's computer crashed earlier as well.'

'And what conclusion do you draw from that, Miss Storm?'

'I'm not quite sure, sir. But something similar happened on the night when the fox – ' she hastily corrected herself – 'when the kitchens burnt down.'

'And you think that both of these fires were caused by some kind of electromagnetic force?' Axford's tone of voice indicated that he thought the idea not a particularly convincing one.

Rebecca paused for a moment, thinking the matter out in her head. 'No,' she said eventually. 'That would be impossible, wouldn't it? But suppose that whatever caused the fires also generated some sort of magnetic field. That would account for the alarm systems being knocked out as well, wouldn't it?'

'It is a possibility,' Axford agreed. 'And what could cause this magnetic field?'

Rebecca shrugged her shoulders. 'A dynamo of some sort?' she suggested. 'Some kind of machine, anyway.'

General Axford drummed his fingers on the top of his desk as he considered the matter. For a moment Rebecca even thought he was taking her seriously.

'So according to you, Miss Storm, persons unknown are operating a machine that can conjure fire out from thin air,' he said. 'Is that what you're saying?'

'Er, I suppose so.'

'First Mr Price here tells me a cock and bull story about ghosts, and now you present me with theories from cheap science fiction movies,' he said. 'That isn't the sort of attitude one expects from Institute students.'

'It's an absurd proposition,' Eva said.

'Indeed,' Axford said. 'And one sadly not confined to children. Take Edward Kesselwood for example.'

'The man was a charlatan and a dreamer,' Eva said, with a vehemence which surprised them.

'Who is Edward Kesselwood?' Rebecca asked. The name rang a vague bell for her. She recalled the name on an old physics text book she'd once read a long time ago.

Axford picked up a framed photograph from his desk and turned it around so that Rebecca, Marc and Colette could see it. It showed a group of five men dressed in military uniform. One of them was clearly Axford, back in the days when he could still walk. She didn't recognise any of the other men.

'He was under my command during the Gulf War,' Axford told them. He pointed out a tall, black-haired figure standing to the left of him. 'A brilliant young physicist, if a little eccentric and misguided.'

'Why would a scientist be working for the army?' Colette asked. As far as she was concerned, science was all about saving life, not destroying it.

'He was employed to develop and improve our weapons systems,' Axford explained. 'Unfortunately he also had some rather unorthodox ideas about the art of warfare.'

'What sort of unorthodox ideas?' Marc wanted to know.

'That is privileged information,' Eva interrupted.

'As Eva says, that is privileged information,' Axford continued. 'In the end I had to dismiss him from the service.' He shook his head sadly. 'Such a waste of an otherwise brilliant scientific mind. It was even more unfortunate when his plane was shot down over the desert on his way back to England.'

'He's dead?' Rebecca asked.

'Of course.'

'Edward Kesselwood is of no concern to us,' Eva said, and for once Marc had to agree with her.

'There have been two fires at the Institute,' he reminded them. 'It's obvious that someone's got it in for us.'

General Axford's brow furrowed. 'Someone deliberately wants to harm the Institute?'

There was genuine concern in his voice now, which was strange because up to now he had seemed perfectly happy to accept the explanation of faulty wiring and even the fact that Marc and Colette had nearly perished in the fire. He looked over at Eva. She was tapping a number out on one of her phones, and it seemed that she was no longer listening to them.

Axford was about to say something else when another of the phones on Eva's desk rang. She answered it and then looked over to Axford. It was for him, she said, and transferred the call to his phone. Marc noticed the small smile on Eva's lips.

Rebecca watched Axford as he spoke to the person on the other end of the line. A worried look appeared in his steel-blue eyes. As he continued speaking, he also developed a nervous tic. When he finally put down the phone, there seemed to be something changed about him.

'That will be all,' he told them abruptly. He was clearly very eager to get rid of them. 'Eva will see you both out.'

'But General, what about the fire?' Rebecca asked, as Eva left her desk and walked over to escort them out of the office.

'That was the police on the telephone,' Axford informed them, as he wheeled himself to the open door. 'The cause of the fire has been determined beyond any doubt.'

'And?' Marc asked. As Eva took his arm to lead him out he shrugged her off and repeated his question. 'What started the fire?'

For an instant Axford hesitated and seemed a little disturbed. It was though he was trying to remember a half-forgotten memory. In that instant Rebecca was shocked to see how vulnerable the man appeared. Then he regained his normal military composure and calmness.

'It seems that one of the computers developed a fault,' Axford told them. 'It shorted and set the whole lab alight.'

'But that's not what happened,' Colette insisted.

'Forget it,' Marc told her. It was clear that neither

Axford nor Eva would believe their version of events.

'You heard what the General said,' Eva interrupted. 'Another electrical fault.'

'We really must have the Institute's entire electrical systems checked,' Axford said wearily, as he steered himself towards the door in his wheelchair.

'General Axford – ' Marc began, but the older man raised a hand to silence him. 'Mr Price!' he said, and now there was no mistaking the clipped military authority in the man's voice. 'An electrical fault! That is an end to the matter!'

'But – '

'You will not concern yourself with the fires again, nor shall you discuss them with your fellow students,' Axford commanded. 'Do you understand?'

'General, that's hardly fair on Marc,' Rebecca said. 'He's only showing a healthy scientific curiosity. "The will to know", I seem to remember you calling it once.'

There was a dangerous moment of tension between Rebecca and Axford, and then the General relaxed and smiled. 'Let us forget all this unpleasantness,' he said.

'We can't forget Joey Williams though, can we?' Colette said without thinking. Rebecca glared at her, but it was too late – the danger was done.

'Who?'

Marc frowned. Did Axford genuinely not know who Joey Williams was?

'He's a new student at the Institute,' Rebecca informed the General. 'Only he hasn't turned up.'

'Except that he *has* turned up but has been kid-napped!' Colette added.

'Eva handles all the admissions to the Institute, ever since my stay in hospital,' Axford reminded them. He looked over at his assistant. 'Have you heard of this boy?'

Eva shook her head. 'No one by that name is known to me,' she declared. 'And I should know, General.'

'But we saw his name on the register,' Rebecca protested.

'You must have been mistaken,' Eva said.

'But there's a kid out there who's being held against his will!' Marc said. 'Don't either of you care?'

Axford turned back to Marc. There was a cold look in his blue eyes, which suggested that, in fact, he really didn't care at all.

'If there is a child missing, then he must be a local child and I suggest that you inform the police,' he stated coldly.

'It should be easy to establish whether he is missing or not,' Eva added. 'There are very few black children living in Brentmouth village, after all.'

Marc chose to ignore the remark. (So contemptuous was he of Eva, that he didn't even stop to think how she could have known that a kid she had never met was black.)

General Axford wheeled himself towards the door. Eva stood up and ushered Marc, Rebecca and Colette out into the corridor. Then she locked the door to the General's office.

'Eva and I have an appointment with the insurance people,' Axford informed them. 'And I'm sure that Miss Russell's tutor will be waiting for her at home.

And you, Miss Storm and Mr Price, have your lessons to attend.'

'Yeah, well, I do have a biology class,' Marc said, looking at his watch.

'And I've my math class, as well,' Rebecca said. She was surprised when she saw the sudden panicky look on Eva's face. It was a look which Rebecca wasn't used to seeing.

'Your mathematics class is . . . cancelled,' Eva informed her curtly.

'Why? Is Dr Molloy ill? She seemed perfectly OK the other day.'

'Dr Molloy resigned from the Institute this morning with immediate effect,' Eva told them. She turned to Axford, who seemed as surprised as the others. 'I was about to inform you, General, when you asked me to collect the children from the hospital.'

'A good teacher,' Axford said, as Eva wheeled him off down the corridor. There was very little emotion in his voice. 'Make sure you find a replacement for her at once, Eva.'

After Axford and Eva had disappeared down the corridor, Rebecca turned back to Marc and Colette. 'I can't believe that Dr Molloy's just left like that,' she said. 'I had no idea that she was even thinking of leaving, when I spoke to her the other day. She certainly never told me anything about it.'

'I'll miss her,' Marc said, as they started to walk off down the corridor. 'She was a sweet old bird. She was as much a part of the Institute as old Axford. A hundred times nicer with it as well.'

'Exactly,' Rebecca said. 'She loved this place; she's spent most of her teaching life here. Why would she suddenly just decide to up and go without telling anyone?'

'What are you suggesting, Rebecca?' Colette asked. 'Do you think she was forced to leave?'

'When I quizzed her about Joseph Williams, she was frightened of something, I'm sure of that. Maybe that's why she left? Otherwise why would she act so oddly?'

'She's not the only one who's acting oddly then.'

'What d'you mean?' Rebecca asked.

'Did you see how Axford changed after he got that phone call from the police forensic team?' Marc asked. 'When I said that someone was out to get the Institute he was really interested. And after the call he looked really scared.'

'Why would General Axford be scared of the police?' asked Colette.

'*If* it was the police on the other end of the line, that is.'

'Of course it was,' Rebecca said sensibly. 'Who else could it be?'

'Bec, for a reasonably intelligent fifteen-year-old, you've got the most trusting nature it's ever been my misfortune to encounter!'

'That's because I look for the best in people, unlike cynical little wusses such as you. Why shouldn't it be the police?'

'The call came through on Axford's private line.'

'How do you know which line it was?' Colette

asked. As far as she was concerned one phone looked very much like another.

'It's the one phone on the desk that isn't connected up to the main switchboard like the others.'

'And?'

That wasn't the complete answer, Rebecca realised. She had known Marc long enough now to realise when he was keeping something from her.

'And a couple of terms ago Axford used that line to ring up my parents when my grades were slipping,' Marc admitted a little shamefacedly. 'I was in his office at the time, getting a proper dressing down . . .'

'That I can believe,' said Rebecca. 'Why didn't I notice that?'

'Because he's the "cynical little wuss" who's got the suspicious nature and you're not?' Colette suggested cheekily.

'Why would he give the police his direct line and not the number of the main switchboard?' Marc asked.

'Search me.'

'Well, I'm going to find out!'

They had now reached the main exit and, as they walked out into the bright May sunshine, they saw the police and the fire brigade who were still moving around the burnt-out shell of the chemistry lab. Liv Farrar was there again, clicking away with her Canon for the school paper. She spotted Marc and waved at him, before carrying on with her work.

'What are you going to do?' Colette asked.

Marc started to walk off to the side of the admin block. 'Trust me, you really don't want to know!' he said. He dived into the pocket of his leather jacket and took out a key which he handed to Rebecca. 'I'll meet you two back in my room in fifteen minutes, OK?'

'OK,' Rebecca sighed, and watched Marc go off. He was probably right, she decided. It would be better for her if she and Colette didn't know what harebrained scheme he was up to.

Their way to the boys' hostel took them past the scene of the fire, and they wandered over to the police barrier which had been erected around what was left of the labs.

'You can't go any further,' a policeman told them, as they approached the cordon.

'It's OK, Officer,' Rebecca said. 'We'll leave you to get on with your job. We were just curious, that's all.'

'You're not the only one who's curious, and I don't mind telling you so,' he said. 'For the life of us, neither we nor the boys from the fire brigade can work out what started this little mess.'

'I thought it was some sort of short circuit?' Colette said.

'To cause this much trouble?' The policeman shook his head. 'No way. Not that forensics could check. The place is a total wipe-out now.'

'But didn't your forensic team give General Axford a ring a few minutes ago?' asked Rebecca.

The policeman appeared puzzled. 'Not as far as I know, Miss. Our people are still trying to work out what started the fire in the first place. Is there anything wrong? You've come over all pale, like.'

Rebecca shook her head. 'No, there's nothing wrong, Officer,' she lied, and found herself looking back at the admin block. Marc's hunch had been right after all, she realised. Whoever had phoned up General Axford, it certainly hadn't been the police.

Dateline: The Institute;
Thursday 10th May; 15.10.

While Rebecca and Colette were talking to the policeman, Marc had sneaked around the back of the admin building, and, after checking that no one was watching, had climbed through the open window into Axford's office.

He wasted no time and crossed over to Eva's desk. He lifted up the receiver of Axford's private line and then punched out a four-digit number. When the recorded voice answered, he scribbled down a number, and then closed the connection.

Keeping an eye on the door, just in case Axford or Eva should unexpectedly return, Marc dialled the new number. The connection was made almost immediately.

He frowned and then put the receiver down.

As he did so he noticed a floptical in Eva's in-tray. He recognised it as the one she had taken from them the other day. He picked it up, slipped it into Eva's computer, and called up a file on-screen. He quickly scrolled down the text file, while he searched in her desk in-tray for a blank floppy.

When he had finished his task, he clicked off the computer, made sure that he'd disturbed nothing in the office, and then went back to the window and climbed out.

Dateline: The Institute, Study Bedroom 101B; Thursday 10th May; 15.24.

Rebecca and Colette were waiting for Marc as arranged in his room in the boys' dorm.

'Marc, you were right,' Rebecca said. 'The police say that they still haven't come up with the cause of that fire. General Axford was lying to us. Whoever rang up it certainly wasn't the police.'

'I know,' Marc said. 'I dialled 1471 on Eva's phone.'

'And?'

'And I called the last number which had rung up.'

'So who was it who called the General?' asked Colette.

'Nobody.'

'What do you mean?' Rebecca asked. 'We saw Axford talking to someone.'

'When I made the connection there was nothing on the other end of the line except for a warbling sound.'

'Warbling sound?' asked Colette.

'Yes. Just like the sound you get when you use your modem to link up with another computer.'

'General Axford was called up by a computer?'

Colette could hardly believe what she was hearing.

'I don't know,' Marc admitted. 'But something shook him up and made him lie to us.' He took the floppy he'd picked up in Axford's office out of his pocket, and handed it to Rebecca.

'What's this?'

'A copy of the list of pupils at the Institute.'

Rebecca frowned. 'So? What use is that going to be?' She stood up and walked across the room to Marc's desk, started up his PC, and inserted the disk.

'I managed to have a quick look at the file while I was in Axford's office,' Marc told her. 'Key up the surnames beginning with "W".'

Rebecca did as she was told. For a moment she didn't quite understand what Marc had in mind. And then she spotted the missing entry.

'Williams, Joseph,' she realised. 'His name's been taken off the list.'

'Suspicious, isn't it?' Marc said. 'Dr Molloy leaves the Institute just as you ask her about this guy. And now his name's been erased from the student roster like he never existed.'

'It could just be another coincidence,' Rebecca suggested, even though she was hardly certain of anything any more.

'Sure it could be,' Marc said. 'Just as it's a coincidence that the real Beltane is only a few days away. Just as it's a coincidence that every time a fireball appears, your electromagnetic experiments up in the physics lab get screwed up. Eva seemed pretty concerned that we shouldn't look at the register. Maybe she knows something about it and she didn't want us to find out about the Williams kid?'

'It still doesn't get us any further in solving the mystery of the fireballs or finding Joey,' Colette said.

'Or who wants to harm the Institute,' added Rebecca.

'We know that the yard seems to be the centre of all the psychic activity,' Marc reminded her.

'So?' Rebecca didn't see where Marc was leading them. 'The police and the fire brigade have searched the yard, and the surrounding buildings, and they haven't come up with anything. Not even a used book of matches.'

'Aha, but maybe they're weren't looking in the right places?'

'What are you talking about, Marc?' Rebecca asked.

'The Institute was built on the site of the nuns' old convent.'

Rebecca groaned. 'Not Sister Uriel again,' she protested. Marc ignored her sarcastic comment.

'I think I know what Marc's talking about,' Colette said. 'Do you remember me saying that there are supposed to be miles of secret tunnels below the Institute?'

'And you think that your nasty nun is down there, haunting the tunnels, and preparing for her reappearance in a few days' time?' Rebecca mocked him.

'Or something's down there. It's worth a look though, isn't it?'

'Just one tiny point,' Rebecca said. 'Even if these tunnels do exist and haven't caved in over the centuries, we have no idea how to get into them.'

Colette looked superiorly at them. 'Oh yes we do!' she said smugly.

Dateline: The Project;
Thursday 10th May; 15.39.

'You fool! Do you want to destroy us all?'

The husky tones of the Deputy Controller of the Project could be heard even in the subterranean laboratory where Joey lay, still strapped to the bench. He struggled to hear the conversation in the passage-way outside.

'The boy was distressed, and couldn't control the Mindfire.' That was White Mask talking and for the first time Joey heard a note of fear in the man's voice.

'And are you surprised? His mind is a mess of confused adolescent emotions.'

'He did lose his sister and mother only recently,' Joey heard White Mask say.

Joey wondered how they knew about Sara and his mother's deaths.

'And we know the effect those traumas had on him,' the Deputy Controller said. 'So why did you tell him about the death of – what was the name of that damnable nurse again?'

'Maria,' White Mask replied.

'Knowing that this Maria is dead only upset him further. Do you wonder why the Mindfire he creates is unstable? Two people were very nearly killed today.'

'I didn't think that you'd be concerned.'

'Their lives are worthless,' the Deputy Controller declared. 'But yet another building was burnt down to the ground. We are drawing attention to ourselves. Even the General is becoming more and more difficult to control.'

'Axford is posing a problem again?' White Mask sounded concerned. 'I thought that had been sorted out several months ago? The accident was meant to put him out of action until we could set up our base here.'

'I dealt with him. A simple subliminal pulse sent down the telephone line, and he stopped asking questions. He is once again under our control.'

'Then you have nothing to worry about.'

'But *you* do, Professor. The Project has paid you a fortune to develop the Mindfire. The Project wants a weapon that is so powerful and precise that it can destroy a thousand Hiroshimas at one stroke or pluck the legs off a fly one by one. And if you can't provide the Project with what it demands, then the Project will have no hesitation in killing you . . .'

Ghost-Hunting

Dateline: Fiveways; Thursday 10th May; 19.13.

'Dad hasn't looked at these old papers for years now,' Colette said, as she brought the dusty cardboard box down from the attic. She started to empty it of its contents. 'These are all the old deeds to the land where the abbey once stood,' she told them. 'Father Kimber was asking my mother about them the other day. He said he could put them on display at next month's church fête. Something about instilling a sense of local history in the community.'

'Funny that,' Rebecca said. 'He's only been here a couple of months. I'd've thought local history would be the least of his interests.'

'I guess he's probably one of these history buffs,' Marc said. 'He was really interested in the layout of

all the old churches and sacred sites in the neighbourhood when we saw him in the belltower of Saint
Michael's.'

'He still didn't know about the Dissolution of the
Monasteries, though,' Colette remarked as she sorted
through the papers. 'I would have thought a priest
would have known it was Henry VIII who was responsible for that.'

Finally she found what she was looking for and
handed a few sheets of old vellum parchments to
Rebecca who studied them briefly, saying, sorry, she
couldn't read Latin. She handed Marc a piece of
brittle-looking parchment which had been folded over
several times. 'Is this what you're looking for?'

Marc carefully unfolded the paper and laid it out
on a table.

'The plans of the old convent,' he said. 'It must have
been in your family for ages.'

'It can't have been hanging around for four hundred
years,' Rebecca scoffed. 'It would have perished by now.'

'It's most probably a copy of a copy.'

He pointed out some of the main topographical
details on the map. Although almost four hundred
years had gone by since the convent had stood on this
site, they could still recognise certain features of the
grounds: a copse of old yew trees here, a small pond
there.

'What's that?' Rebecca asked. She drew their
attention to a tiny blue line on the map which weaved
its way from the pond towards the cloisters which
stood in the centre of the convent.

'A stream of some sort.' Colette suggested.

'Well, that proves that the map is wrong,' Rebecca said. 'There's nothing there now.'

'Bec, the original map is about four hundred years old!' Marc said. 'The stream's probably still running somewhere underground.'

'And do you have any proof for that wild assumption?'

'When did I ever need proof?' Marc grinned, before adding: 'Well, at least I haven't got any proof yet!' He turned back to Colette. 'Have you got a PhotoShop program and a scanner?'

'A what?' Colette looked mystified. 'Dad's got a computer in his study if that's what you mean. He uses it for all his CompuDisk business.'

Marc chuckled. He'd forgotten that when it came to modern technology, Colette's knowledge was practically zilch. 'Never mind,' he said. 'Liv Farrar will have a PhotoShop program and a scanner back at the girls' hostel. She uses it for editing the school newspaper.'

'What possible use could they be to you?'

'Practically indispensable,' he said, 'especially when you're going out ghost-hunting!'

Dateline: The Institute;
Thursday 10th May; 21.19.

It was now only a matter of hours before Uriel's scheduled appearance. Even the sceptical Rebecca had to admit that the nun had chosen the right moment to return. The May weather had taken a turn for the worse, and a storm was on its way.

By the time they had flashed their ID cards at the porter in his security hut, signed Colette in, and reached Marc's study bedroom on the third floor, dark clouds were rolling in.

Colette looked out of the window and saw a streak of lightning flash out of the sky, hitting the spire of Saint Michael's church down in Brentmouth village.

'I hope Father Kimber's all right,' she said. 'If he's up on the belltower with his telescope, who knows what might happen?'

'It's the start of Uriel's vengeance,' Marc said half-jokingly, as he played around with his own Apple Mac. 'She's bound to have it in for old Kimber. She probably wants to make sure that he won't come and perform an exorcism!'

'You really think so?' Colette asked, not quite sure whether Marc was making fun of her or not.

'Pay no attention to him, Colette,' Rebecca said and laughed. 'The lightning's simply attracted by the lightning conductor on the church spire. That way it just travels harmlessly down to the ground.'

'You're no fun, Bec!' Marc called them both over to the Apple Mac. They peered over his shoulder at the image he'd brought up on screen.

'That's a map of the Institute,' Rebecca said.

'That's right,' Marc said. 'I used Liv's computer to scan and Photoshop it from the map they gave us in the school prospectus.'

'You spent a long time in her room,' Colette remarked innocently. 'I don't understand why Rebecca and I had to wait outside.'

'Er, her system crashed and we had problems rebooting it,' Marc said hastily.

'I bet,' said Rebecca.

Marc pointed out the main buildings, the admin block and the places where the chemistry lab and the kitchen annexe had stood before the fires.

'Now take a look at this.'

He opened up another file and called up a copy he'd made of the old map of the convent. He double clicked with the mouse, and overlaid that map on to the one of the Institute. He jabbed a finger at the screen.

'See, that's the course of the stream,' he said, 'and it goes straight to the cloisters of the old abbey.'

'So?'

'Use your eyes, Bec,' he said. 'The yard is built directly above the cloisters – the place where Uriel worshipped, and where she was probably bricked up and left to die!'

In spite of her cynicism, Rebecca felt a chill run down her spine. 'It still doesn't prove anything,' she said. 'And it certainly doesn't prove that part of the old convent is still buried underground.'

'No, but we can find out,' Marc crowed. He pointed to a small circle on the Institute map.

'What's that?'

'It's the old well,' Marc told her. Rebecca remembered being told that it had been boarded up years ago. Something about local kids using it as a hiding place, she recalled.

Rebecca stared wide-eyed at Marc as she suddenly realised what he was considering. Of all Marc's crazy schemes, this one was the limit!

'You can't be serious,' she said.

'Sure I am,' he said, as casually as if he was just planning a day-outing to the seaside. 'If I can get down that well, then I can see if it leads into the tunnels that Colette's so sure exist down there.'

'I only said that some people *thought* there were tunnels,' Colette corrected him.

'It's too dangerous, Marc,' Rebecca protested. 'You could get yourself killed. If there really are tunnels down there, then they could cave in at any time. If – '

Marc told her to be silent. 'If, if, if,' he mocked. 'If I don't go down there then we'll never know if all this is the work of some supernatural force or not. If I don't go down there, we may never know what happened to Joey Williams,' he continued, before adding slyly, 'C'mon, Bec, you're always saying I talk a load of nonsense. Give me the chance to prove that you're right!'

'You can't, Marc,' Colette said. 'It's far too dangerous.'

'I'm not asking you to come with me.'

'But – '

'You're far too young,' he said, and Colette saw red. Before she could say anything, Rebecca interrupted.

'Isn't there one thing you're forgetting, Marc?'

'There is?'

'You're acting on impulse again, and you haven't thought things through. How are we – '

'We?'

'Someone's got to look after you, haven't they?' she replied. 'How are we going to knock out the security systems and cameras?'

'What security cameras?' asked Colette. 'I didn't see any when we came here to Marc's room.'

'Eva had them installed around the main part of the Institute a few months ago,' Marc explained. 'You should know. It was your dad's company that provided them.'

'Dad never tells me anything,' Colette said sadly. 'Why would Eva want to install security around just one part of the Institute?'

'Why does Eva do so many things?' asked Marc. 'She follows her own agenda. But we do know the security system is switched on every night.'

Colette still didn't see what the problem was. 'So why not go down the well during the day?' she asked.

'And get caught by Eva?' Marc said. 'No, we have to do it at night. But how do we disable the security systems?'

'It would be easy if we knew the security codes,' Rebecca said, and looked thoughtfully at the modem beside Marc's computer. She turned back to Colette. 'Colette, you have to go home.'

Colette shook her head. 'I'm not a little girl, you know,' she said defiantly. 'If you're going out looking for Uriel and Joey then I want to help you.'

'And you will by going home,' Rebecca told her. 'Now here's my plan . . .'

Dateline: The Institute;
Thursday 10th May; 22.25.

'Thanks anyway, Colette,' Rebecca said, and put the telephone receiver down and walked sadly back to Marc's room. He looked up expectantly when she came in.

'Any luck?' he asked.

'That was Colette back at Fiveways,' she told him and handed him a piece of paper. 'Here's the number of her father's modem. But she says that she doesn't know the password.'

'So the number's useless. We need to know the password to get into his computer and find the access codes for the Institute's security system,' Marc said. Nevertheless he tapped the number into his own computer. The modem gave out a warbling sound, before linking up with Mr Russell's computer, which Rebecca had told Colette to switch on.

The words >**PLEASE ENTER PASSWORD** appeared on the screen.

'It'll be a word that's important to him, and one that's also easy to remember,' Rebecca knew, and suggested a few possibilities to Marc: the name of the Russells' house; the brand names of some of the products produced by CompuDisk Ltd. Each and every attempt ended with the words >**SORRY, ACCESS DENIED**.

Marc sat back in his chair and sighed. 'Neat idea,

Bec,' he said. 'Just a shame there are about a million possible passwords out there.' In an act of desperation he keyed in the name >URIEL. Still access was denied to them.

'You'd be surprised how often people use the names of people they love as their passwords,' Rebecca said. She reached over and tapped out a name on the keyboard.

>ACCESS APPROVED.

'Well done, Bec!' Marc cheered. 'What word did you key in?'

Rebecca smiled and pointed to the name on the screen: >COLETTE.

Marc grinned. 'Well, well, well. It looks as though her dad does love her after all!'

Dateline: Fiveways; Thursday 10 May; 22.33.

Colette stared out of her bedroom window at Saint Michael's in the distance. Forks of lightning illuminated the night sky, as they travelled down to the lightning conductor on the church roof.

She shivered. She couldn't get Joey out of her mind. There was a deep throbbing in her head, as though he were trying to reach out to her. There was some sort of psychic link between the two of them, of that she was sure. Then why couldn't she contact him as he had contacted her? She slammed her fist into the palm of her hand in frustration.

Not only was she worried about Joey, she was concerned for Marc and Rebecca as well. If they did find the hidden tunnels then would they meet up with Uriel? Father Kimber had warned them all that Uriel's vengeance would be terrible if they persisted in interfering with things they knew nothing about. Were Marc and Rebecca in terrible danger?

Finally Colette came to a decision. She had to get help.

But who to turn to? Her dad was still away on another business trip to the States, her mother was at yet another of her women's meetings, and Miss Kerr certainly wouldn't believe stories of vengeful spirits.

No, there was only one person in the whole of Brentmouth who would take her seriously.

Colette slipped into her coat and headed off towards Saint Michael's church. Father Kimber would know what to do, she was sure of that.

Dateline: Saint Michael's Church;
Thursday 10 May; 23.14.

'I thought I told you not to interfere with the forces of darkness!'

Father Kimber had exploded when Colette had told him about Marc and Rebecca's ghost-hunting expedition. She had found the parish priest in a small room just off the nave. He was poring over some old maps, and studying a diagram on a large piece of paper.

When she had entered through the door, he had hastily covered up his work.

'But it's not just Uriel they're interested in now,' Colette said. 'It's Joey as well.'

'Joey?'

'He's a boy who was supposed to come to the Institute, but he was kidnapped.'

'A young boy,' Father Kimber said, almost to himself. He stroked his chin thoughtfully. 'Yes, they would need a child after all . . .The mind of an adult would not be as sensitive to the forces in the earth . . .'

'Father, what are you talking about?'

Father Kimber fixed Colette with a steely glare. 'You must not interfere with the powers of evil. Leave Uriel alone.'

'Then Marc and Rebecca really are in danger down those tunnels?'

'What tunnels?' Kimber demanded and gripped Colette's arm tightly.

'The tunnels of the old convent,' she said. 'Marc said he thought that you could reach them through a well in the Institute grounds.'

'They still exist?'

'We're not sure,' Colette said. 'Please, let go of my arm – you're hurting me.'

Father Kimber released his grip, and apologised. 'The old abbey,' he muttered to himself. 'Yes, they could be there.' He uncovered the maps and diagrams he had been working on, and started to study them.

'What are those, Father?' Colette asked.

'Nothing to trouble you, my child,' he said and

continued to examine them. He started to chuckle. 'How could I have been so foolish? And so near the Institute as well!'

'I don't understand,' Colette said as Father Kimber folded up the papers and stood up.

'Come along, my child,' he said. 'You must show me where the well leading to the tunnels is. It is time to confront the forces of evil head-on.'

'Sister Uriel, you mean?'

'If you like.' Father Kimber walked into the main body of the church. 'Colette, wait for me outside,' he said. 'If I am to do battle with evil, then I must prepare myself.'

'I understand, Father,' Colette said and left to allow the priest to pray in silence.

When she had gone, Father Kimber didn't kneel down in front of the altar to pray as Colette had supposed he would do.

Instead, he produced a small gold key and opened the tiny tabernacle behind the altar. Inside lay a loaded revolver. Father Kimber quickly took it out and hid it in the pocket of his coat, before meeting up outside with Colette.

THE PSYCHIC ZONE

12

Uriel

Dateline: The Institute;
Thursday 10th May; 23.30.

'I must be out of my mind to help you, Marc Price,' Rebecca said, as she stood before the old boarded-up well, dressed in her warmest clothing. The well was in its own little copse of small trees and brambles, half-hidden just by the inside of the Institute walls. In the sky the storm was breaking and rain was starting to come down in sheets.

'No, you're not out of your mind. You want to know what's behind all this as much as I do. That's why you're here.'

'If the General or Eva finds us, there'll be all hell to pay . . .' Rebecca said. She looked nervously back at the Institute building. There were a few lights shining in the windows.

'Well, let's hope they don't,' he said, and opened the rucksack he was carrying. 'With the security system down we should be OK.'

He took out a long length of rope which he looped over his shoulder; a pair of torches, one of which he handed to Rebecca, and the other which he slipped into the pocket of his leather jacket and an iron crowbar. He also handed her a compass. The needle was pointing to magnetic north, as usual.

'Why do you need a compass?' Rebecca asked, as Marc started to prise the wooden boards from off the top of the covered well.

'All the fires so far have been accompanied by some kind of electromagnetic force,' Marc reminded her. 'So if Uriel has got anything to do with them and she's about to put in an appearance, then this compass should give us an early warning.' He wrenched away at the last of the wooden planks covering the mouth of the well.

'Well done,' Rebecca said. 'You did that in record time!'

'Pulling things apart is one of my specialities, Bec!' Marc said, and dropped the crowbar to the ground. 'Still, they gave way much easier than I thought.'

'They were probably just damp and rotten.'

'Not rotten,' Marc said. 'Dried out, if anything.'

He took the torch out of his leather jacket, and shone it down into the well. Rebecca joined him in looking over the edge.

'Spooky, isn't it?' he said with relish as he peered into the blackness.

He picked up a heavy stone and dropped it into the well. They waited a couple of seconds and then heard the stone thud into dry earth.

'The well must have dried up years ago,' Rebecca guessed.

Marc took the length of rope off his shoulders and tied one end around his waist. He handed the other end to Rebecca.

'There seem to be some kind of rungs set into the brickwork. I'm going to try to use those to get down.'

'Be careful,' Rebecca said, as Marc swung his legs over the edge of the well. 'Those rungs could be rusty.'

'They should be able to bear my weight. And if not the rope should stop me from falling.'

'I'll tie my end around this tree.' Rebecca looped the rope around a low-hanging and sturdy branch of one of the yew trees which overlooked the well.

Marc set a foot on the topmost rung, and pressed down experimentally with his weight. The rung seemed to be fixed securely enough to the wall and only gave a little.

'OK, Bec, wish me luck,' he said. Since he would be needing the use of both of his hands, he attached the lit torch to his belt. At least that would give him some illumination on the way down.

'Give my love to Uriel.'

'Very funny,' Marc said, and disappeared down into the well.

The air was dry and musty, smelling of dead leaves. It was warm too, Marc noticed, as he carefully made his way down the rungs. That was hardly surprising though; he was going underground after all.

Marc was about halfway down, when he placed his foot on a rung which wasn't as securely fastened to the walls as the others. It gave beneath his weight, and he swayed horribly for a moment, before losing his balance. Frantically he reached out for another handhold.

On the surface the rope suddenly grew taut with Marc's weight. Rebecca pulled at it with all her strength, in a vain attempt to halt Marc's fall.

It was no use – Marc was far too heavy. Rebecca looked gratefully at the old yew tree. Thank God she'd had the good sense to attach the rope to the branch. *At least that should hold Marc's weight*, she thought.

She was wrong. The branch snapped under all of Marc's fifty-four kilos, and Rebecca watched on in horror as the rope was ripped out of her hands. It followed Marc down into the well.

Rebecca ran over to the well and shone her torch down into its inky blackness. There was no reply. Without any concern for her own safety, she swung a leg over the edge.

It took her just over a minute to reach the bottom. She would have been quicker, but she had been careful to test every rung carefully before she set her foot on it. She needn't have worried. Marc had been right and most of the rungs were securely fastened to the wall. *It was just his bad luck to step on a dodgy one*, she reflected.

The bottom of the well was dark and dusty. When Rebecca switched on her torch, she heard the skittering sound of mice as they ran away from the beam of light.

She heard groaning and shone her light into the far corner. Marc was lying there, half-conscious, and she darted over to him, and shook him fully awake.

'Are you OK?'

Marc came to, and Rebecca helped him to sit up. 'What happened?' he asked groggily, as he searched on the ground for his torch. It had fallen off his belt and gone out when he'd hit the bottom.

'You fell.'

'Obviously,' Marc looked at the tangled rope which lay on the ground. 'What happened to it?'

'The branch of the tree broke,' Rebecca told him. 'I don't understand it. It seemed so strong; I thought it could hold you . . .'

'Well, it didn't,' he said ruefully and tried to stand up. He moaned; he was aching all over. He clicked on the torch and shone it around the walls of the well. There was a gap in the wall, about two metres high and roughly a metre wide. He gave Rebecca a triumphant look.

'See, I was right after all. That's the tunnel that follows the course of the old stream.'

'Marc, it's just a crack in the wall,' Rebecca said as she peered inside.

'It opens up further on into a tunnel,' he told her. 'It'll take us right into the ruins of the convent.' He started to move towards the tunnel opening but Rebecca held him back.

'Marc, I don't like this.'

'Scared? *You*? Of Sister Uriel?'

'Of course not,' Rebecca said indignantly. 'I just

don't think it's safe, that's all. Those tunnel walls and roof could collapse at any second.'

'Come on, Bec, they've been standing for over four hundred years now.' He moved towards the tunnel entrance again. Rebecca followed reluctantly.

Although it was a tight fit, after only a few paces the tunnel opened up considerably and they were able to stand up straight.

Marc shone his torch on to the arched roof. It seemed to be supported by stone pillars, decorated with elaborate carvings of men and animals. They reminded Marc of the ones he'd seen once on a day trip to Westminster Abbey. There was something sinister about them as well.

'This can't just be the course of the old stream, after all,' he said. 'This has to be the route that Uriel took when she was after her bit of how's-your-father with her abbot.'

'Don't be vulgar,' Rebecca said, but smiled in the darkness. At least Marc's flip remark had helped to cheer things up.

Marc turned his torch on to one of the statues on the pillars. The harsh white light cast weird shadows, making the stone carvings even more threatening than they already were.

'Ugly so and so, aren't you?' he said as he examined one small gargoyle which was staring malevolently back at him.

'Marc, let's go.' Rebecca loosened the top of her jacket. 'Haven't you noticed the temperature? It's getting warmer.'

"Course it is,' Marc said, trying to hide his growing concern from his voice. 'We're underground, that's why.'

Rebecca shook her head and literally put her foot down. 'Sorry, Marc, I'm not moving a step further,' she declared.

Marc turned around. 'You stay here then,' he said, and showed her where the tunnel bent sharply and led off in another direction. 'Give me five minutes and then I'll come back.'

Rebecca wasn't so sure, but finally agreed to the plan. After he'd been gone for little over a minute, but which, for Rebecca in the darkness, seemed like hours, she shone her torch on to her watch to check the time. She frowned. Her watch had stopped.

She loosened the shirt around her neck. A thin line of sweat trickled down her brow. She had been right. It was getting hotter by the second. She touched the brick wall at her side – what should have been cold and clammy to the touch now felt warm.

Rebecca looked back down the tunnel Marc had taken, and called after him. There was no reply. She thought of following him, when she heard a noise coming from behind her. The sound of approaching footsteps. Rebecca was about to click off her torch when the figure stepped into the beam of light.

'Colette! You gave me the fright of my life! What are you doing down here?'

Then she saw Father Kimber bringing up the rear.

'Where is Marc?' he demanded.

Rebecca frowned. When she'd met Kimber at the

cottage hospital he'd seemed an engaging and dod-
dery character. Yet the man now before her seemed to
carry about him an air of undisputed authority.

'He's gone off down the tunnel.'

'I warned you to stay away,' Father Kimber said. 'I
told you not to interfere with Uriel.'

'Come off it!' Rebecca said scornfully. 'You surely
don't believe in all this nonsense, too, do you?'

Father Kimber smiled a strange smile, and was
about to say something when Rebecca's torch went
out with a popping sound. All three of them were
plunged into darkness. Colette grabbed tight hold of
Rebecca's arm.

'What's happened?'

'Blasted torch has cut out on me.'

'It's more than that.' Kimber's voice was low and
sombre in the darkness. 'Can't you feel it? It's getting
hotter . . .'

Colette's grip on Rebecca's arm increased. 'It's
Uriel, I know it is,' she said. 'You were right, Father,
we shouldn't have got ourselves involved.'

The heat was becoming overbearing. There was a
strange smell in the air, a sharp electric tang. It was
getting hard to breathe.

Kreeee . . .

Rebecca and Colette froze at the dreaded sound. It
increased in volume until it was so loud that chips of
stone and plaster started to tumble from the ceiling to
the ground.

Still it grew louder. The ground seemed to shake
beneath the two girls' feet. Rebecca felt her flesh tingle,

and she could have sworn that her hair was standing on end. Colette's head started to hurt.

Beside them, Father Kimber stood stock still, betraying no emotion whatsoever. In the half-light he looked like a man waiting for something.

Kreeee . . .

'It's Uriel,' Colette said.

'Don't be ridiculous, Colette!' Rebecca snapped.

By now the whole tunnel was shaking. If Rebecca hadn't known any better she would have said that they were in the middle of a minor earthquake. And that was impossible here in the English countryside – wasn't it?

Kreeee . . .

'She said she'd return and now she has!' Colette realised.

Father Kimber still remained silent.

And then the entire tunnel was suddenly filled with a dazzling light. It was so brilliant that Rebecca and Colette had to shield their eyes from its savage glare. For several horrible moments, their bones were visible through the skin of their outstretched hands. Rebecca looked over at Father Kimber. There was a wild smile on his face.

'At last,' she heard him mutter. 'At last!'

Something had appeared in front of them. Something evil. Something unnatural. Something *alien.*

'Now do you believe me and Marc?' Colette asked.

At first Rebecca tried to make herself think that she was imagining it. Then she suspected that she could be witnessing some weird but perfectly natural phenomenon. And then she finally gave in and realised that she had to believe the evidence of her own eyes.

About two metres away from them, and floating about half a metre off the ground, was – not a ball of fire – but a single, brilliantly white flame.

Only it wasn't a flame at all. Well, at least not like any flame any of them had ever seen before.

Although it flickered and faltered in mid-air as it made its way slowly towards them, Rebecca could see a shape concealed in the fire. She could clearly make out the figure's arms and legs. She could see its face screaming in its final agonies.

Rebecca was looking at the face of Sister Uriel – Sister Uriel who had finally returned to take her vengeance on them all.

13

Mindfire

Dateline: The Institute;
Thursday 10th May; 21.19.

The tunnel Marc had taken ended in a dead-end.
Blocking his way was a pile of rubble, the remains of
a collapsed wall. Realising that Rebecca was probably
right and that the tunnels weren't quite as safe as they
appeared (not that he'd ever admit that to her, of
course), he decided to give up and return the way he
had come.

Suddenly the light from his torch started to fade.
Then it went out completely. Willing himself not to
panic, he reached into his pockets for the lighter he
usually carried.

He snapped it on and the flame flickered in the
darkness – there was probably a breeze somewhere –
but it did provide him with enough light to retrace

the way he had come. Suddenly Colette's shriek of terror came from the other end of the tunnel. Wasting no more time, he raced off in the direction of her scream.

The entire tunnel was now filled with a weird, unearthly light. Marc turned the corner and shielded his eyes from the brilliance of the blazing figure of Sister Uriel, suspended in mid-air.

Every second she was coming closer to Rebecca and Colette, who seemed frozen to the spot, like rabbits caught in the path of an oncoming car. Father Kimber was standing there, watching the approaching demon with a mixture of horror and fascination.

Up to now even Marc had never quite believed in the legend of Uriel. There had always been a small niggling doubt in the back of his mind that maybe he was being just a bit too imaginative for his own good. Yet now here was the proof, seen by his very own eyes. This was real.

Father Kimber dropped to his knees by Colette's side, and, for one bizarre moment, Marc thought he was going to pray for deliverance from Uriel. Then he watched as the man shook Colette by the shoulders.

'Concentrate!' he said.

'I don't understand,' Colette said. She could feel the heat on her face now, and the hot air was burning her lungs. 'It's Uriel . . .'

'Don't be stupid, child, there is no such thing as Uriel!' Father Kimber snapped.

'Then what's that?' Rebecca cried. Uriel was nearly on top of them now.

'The Mindfire is taking on the appearance of what's in the child's mind!' Kimber had to shout to make himself heard above the crackling and spluttering of the fire. 'It's created by the mind – and it can be altered and destroyed by the mind as well.'

'I don't understand,' Colette cried.

'Concentrate, child!' Father Kimber shouted. 'Make the Mindfire smaller. Concentrate! Sister Uriel does not exist! Say it over to yourself. Sister Uriel does not exist!'

Colette stared into the heart of the fire, willing Sister Uriel to disappear. For long seconds, nothing happened; if anything, the flaming form of Uriel grew larger and brighter.

'Concentrate, Colette! Concentrate!'

And then the flame started to flicker and falter. It lost its shape. No longer did it have the appearance of a vengeful nun. Now it was a ball of fire, which rapidly shrank, until it finally blipped out of existence.

Colette and Rebecca both breathed a huge sigh of relief, and Marc came running over to them. Colette was pale and she was shivering. The mental ordeal had obviously taken a lot out of her. Father Kimber stood up and looked in the direction from which Marc had come.

'What's back there?' he asked.

'Colette is feeling weak,' Rebecca said. 'We must get her out of here.'

'What's back there?' the parish priest repeated his question.

'Don't you care about Colette?' Marc asked angrily.

'There's nothing back there. It's a dead-end.'

'There must be something,' Father Kimber said. 'The Mindfire is very near.'

'I don't know what you're talking about,' Rebecca said, 'but we're getting out of here.'

'No, you're not,' Kimber stated.

'Try and stop us,' Rebecca said, and gasped as Father Kimber pulled the revolver from out of his jacket, and trained it on them. He smiled sarcastically at them.

'Please don't make me use it,' he said. 'I've no wish to hurt you.'

'You're not a priest at all,' Colette realised.

'Obviously not,' Kimber replied.

'I should have guessed when you made that slip-up about the Dissolution of the Monasteries,' Marc realised.

'But what are you doing at Saint Michael's?' Colette asked, though Kimber chose to ignore her question.

'Now shall we see what lies at the other end of the tunnel?' he said.

Dateline: The Project;
Thursday 10th May; 21.19.

'I told you, it's a dead-end,' Marc said after Kimber had escorted them down the tunnel at gunpoint.

The older man's face fell, and he lowered his revolver.

'But there must be,' Kimber said. 'All the triangulations point to this area.'

'Triangulations?' Colette said, and remembered the maps and diagrams she'd spotted back at the church.

'You said you could contact this Williams child,' Kimber said.

'No, I said that I could hear his voice in my head,' Colette corrected him.

'And can you hear it now?'

'No.'

Marc looked thoughtfully at the rubble at the dead-end of the tunnel. 'When I was here before my torch conked out on me.'

'The effect of the Mindfire or whatever – or whoever – is powering it,' Kimber said.

'So I used my lighter to find my way around.'

'A lighter?' Rebecca asked. 'You haven't started smoking, have you?'

'Don't be daft,' Marc said. 'I use it in my chemistry class to light the Bunsens, that's all. And when I used my lighter in the tunnel, the flame started to flicker.'

'Just like our torches then. Only the problem wasn't electromagnetics, but too little gas.'

'No, I'd bought the lighter that morning at the same time I bought the new batteries for the torches.'

'But then that means air must be coming in from somewhere!' said Colette.

Kimber excitedly swung the beam of his torch up towards the ceiling. Sure enough, there was a small gap between the rubble and the ceiling. He tried to clear away the rubble but the debris proved too heavy to move. He looked at Colette.

'You must go through,' he said, and pointed to the cleft in the wall. 'You're small enough to squeeze through.'

'No, she won't,' Rebecca said. 'Why should she do what you tell her to do?'

'We must have the Mindfire!' Kimber stated.

'We don't even know who you really are,' Rebecca said.

'The disguise was necessary,' Kimber said. 'It enabled me to blend in with the village, so I could carry out my work undisturbed. Just as my warning you of the dangers of Uriel was meant to keep you away from interfering with my investigations.'

'Investigations?' Marc asked.

'Into the ley-lines and the Mindfire,' he continued, and Marc remembered his first conversation with the so called priest in the belltower of Saint Michael's. Invisible lines of power, criss-crossing the country like a giant spider's web.

'Colette must go through. We must find the Project's base!'

'The Project?' asked Rebecca. 'What's the Project?' Kimber ignored her. All he was really interested in was persuading Colette to climb through the gap in the wall.

'We don't know what's behind there,' Marc said, but Colette had already started climbing up the rubble and towards the opening.

'We'll soon find out, won't we?' Colette asked.

'Maybe Joey is there.' There was a new authority in her voice, which Marc and Rebecca had never heard before.

'Marc's right, Colette,' said Rebecca. 'It could be dangerous.'

'You don't understand,' Colette said. 'Joey needs me. Ever since his sister died I'm the only friend he's had. I have to help him.'

And without any further ado, Colette squeezed herself into the opening and disappeared.

Dateline: The Project;
Thursday May 10th; 23.46.

It was a tight fit, but Colette managed to ease herself through the narrow gap between the roof and the pile of rubbish. When she'd climbed through, she found herself in a large passageway. Stone pillars lined the wall. Malevolent gargoyles stared down at her.

She'd come out in the old convent, she realised, buried and forgotten now for hundreds of years. This was the place where Sister Uriel was tracked down by her pursuers and killed.

The whole place reeked of corruption and decay. Colette shuddered as she imagined what Uriel must have felt as the last brick was placed in the wall and she was doomed to a painful and lingering death.

Although she had taken Rebecca's torch she discovered that she didn't need it. Several old-fashioned

torches had been set up on the walls, and their flicker-
ing flames cast eerie shadows down the passageway.

There was another light too, a greenish artificial
light coming from a large chamber.

Colette!

'Who's there?' Colette turned around.

I knew you'd come.

Joey's voice echoed in her mind.

Don't talk. Speak to me with your thoughts . . .

'My thoughts?' Colette whispered. 'I don't understand.'

You must help me . . .

Colette walked towards the green light, keeping to
the walls of the passageway so she wouldn't be seen
by whoever – or whatever – White Mask was. She
could hear a slight humming, and there was a tart tang
to the air.

Kreeee . . .

Colette entered the chamber and realised that she
was in the cloisters of the buried abbey. The first thing
she saw was Joey, strapped to the bench. The helmet
on his head twinkled with a myriad of little lights,
and it was connected to a huge bank of monitors, a
series of large computers, and one large dynamo –
the purpose of which Colette could never hope to
guess. One screen showed a series of dots, joined
together by red lines. Colette recognised the relative
positions of the Darkfell Rise, Saint Michael's, Saint
Wulfrida's out at Fetchwood and the Institute itself –
all of them built on the pathways of Father Kimber's
ley-lines.

All this hi-tech equipment looked strangely out of place in these medieval cloisters. More than that. It was almost blasphemous, a once-holy place being used for the forces of evil like this.

Colette ran towards Joey, anxious to untie the leather straps and get him out of this terrible place as fast as she could.

No, Colette!

Joey's warning came too late. A figure darted from out of the shadows.

Oh, shame!

Colette froze as soon as she saw Omar come towards her. She looked frantically around. There was a stone door at the far end of the chamber, but she'd never reach it in time. The only other exit was the way in which she'd come. And the cruel looking thug would easily out-run her.

Nevertheless, it was her one and only chance. With one final look at Joey – *Sorry,* she thought; *Yeah, sure* came back the reply – she turned and ran.

'Leave her,' another voice said.

Omar stopped and walked up to join his master.

White Mask strolled calmly over to the control console by Joey's bench. He flicked a few levers; he activated several touch-sensitive controls; adjusted a number of dials. The lights on Joey's helmet started to burn brighter. By the time Colette was halfway down the passage, the earth had started to shake, and that dreaded sound had returned, but even louder this time.

Kreeee . . .

Joey squirmed in his bonds. 'Don't make me do it! Not her!'

Joey's protests went unheeded. As soon as Colette had reached the passageway, sheets of flame sprang out of nowhere, circling her in their fiery embrace. She was trapped in a ring of flame.

'Kill her. Use the Mindfire to kill her now!'

'Noooooo . . .' Joey moaned, and he screwed his eyes up trying to concentrate, trying to will the fire away from Colette.

Colette fell to her knees as the flames grew nearer. Sweat poured from her forehead. Her skin tingled with the heat of the Mindfire.

Help me, Joey! Colette cried out as she started to lose consciousness. *Help me now!*

Perhaps it was because Colette had reached out her mind to Joey and in doing so had strengthened his psychic powers. Perhaps it was simply because Joey wouldn't allow White Mask to use him to kill Colette. Whatever the reason, the flames circling Colette started to dance away from her, and then separated from each other, before joining up once again in a single ball of flame.

Get away, Colette, get away while you can!

The fireball was between Colette and the gap in the wall, so the only thing she could do was return to White Mask's lab. As she crossed the cloister floor, the ball of light started slowly to follow her.

White Mask slapped Joey in the mouth. Linked as she was to Joey's own mind, Colette too felt his pain.

'You will obey the Project!' White Mask barked. He

adjusted another control on the command console by the bench.

'No! No!'

The fireball stopped in mid-air for a moment, and spluttered. And then, fuelled by Joey's mental anguish, it exploded into an enormous ball of whitehot flame.

**THE
PSYCHIC
ZONE**

14

Beltane

Dateline: The Institute; Beltane; 00.00.

Marc and Rebecca looked anxiously at the dead-end wall, wondering what had happened to Colette. They turned back to Kimber. He seemed to be as anxious as them.

'What is behind that wall?' Marc asked.

'The Mindfire,' Kimber said. 'It's all seems so obvious now. The ley-lines in this part of the country all converge here. Imagine the power that might be contained in the earth at this very spot.'

'Lines of geomagnetic force meeting at a central point,' Rebecca realised. 'But no one can just tap into power like that. It's not something you turn on and off.'

'I cannot,' Kimber said. 'But imagine if there was

someone who could. Someone with the mental capacity to unlock that energy and channel it as they see fit. Imagine the military consequences. Tongues of white-hot fire destroying the enemy's defences. Balls of flame, hotter than the sun, seeking out their missiles. Fire that comes from nowhere and which can incinerate whole cities.'

'That's sick,' she said. 'And that's the Mindfire? That's the power you want to control?'

'The government wants to ensure that the Project does not control it,' Kimber said.

'You never did tell us what the Project is,' Marc said.

Kimber was about to answer when –

Kreeee . . .

Marc acted with split-second reflexes. He heard a massive *whoompf*, and pushed Rebecca and Kimber down to the ground. There was an explosion, which blew open the blocked doorway.

A sheet of flame scorched above their heads before vanishing, leaving behind a foul and acrid smell. Part of the ceiling came tumbling down. Rebecca screamed, fearing that the whole tunnel would crash on top of them.

As soon as the dust had cleared, Marc leapt up to his feet, and dragged Rebecca with him. He made his way to the gaping hole which Joey's out-of-control fireball had made.

'Come on,' Marc said and headed towards the green light at the end of the passageway. 'We have to find Colette!'

Rebecca looked back at Kimber. A large chunk of the ceiling had fallen down on him, and he was already struggling to move it off.

'What about Kimber?'

'Colette first!' Marc said. He ran off down the passageway and into White Mask's laboratory.

'Well, well, well, more unwelcome visitors,' White Mask said as they burst into the room.

Marc sighed. White Mask and Omar were pointing guns at them. He turned to Rebecca. 'Somehow I don't think this is turning out to be the best Beltane I've ever had.'

'Don't joke! I'm scared stiff!'

'And you honestly think that I'm not?'

White Mask motioned the two of them to join Colette who was standing by the command console. When Rebecca saw Joey on the bench, wide-eyed and frightened, she turned angrily on White Mask.

'What are you doing to him?' she demanded. Marc asked. 'What's he got to do with all these fireballs and Uriel?'

'Uriel?' The name meant nothing to White Mask. 'Joseph is a mere tool, a conductor of energies . . .'

'A conductor?' Rebecca thought back to the lightning conductor on the top of Saint Michael's in the village.

'Joseph is able to tap the invisible lines of energy that cross the whole of this planet,' he told them, 'and focus them as we see fit. Focus them to create all-consuming fire from out of the air, or to score patterns on a tiny lump of tungsten.'

'Just like a human battery,' Colette realised. Was that what Joey now was? Just a tool in the hands of this maniac?

'You haven't been very successful so far, have you?' Rebecca sneered. 'You've almost burnt down the Institute more than once.'

'There will be . . . accidents . . . until Williams can control the Mindfire properly,' White Mask said. 'Just as there were problems back in the Middle East. The children we used there were consumed by the Mindfire as they lost control of the energies buried deep within the earth.'

'Middle East?' Rebecca remembered Colette's father had been over there to look into the security aspect of some oilfields after mysterious fires. 'Were they also the product of the Mindfire?'

'And how do you know all this?' Marc demanded.

'The Project knows many things,' White Mask crowed. 'And now the Project will put that power to its best use!'

'That's enough, Kesselwood,' a voice came from the entrance to the chamber. 'You can give yourself up now.'

Marc and Rebecca looked at each other in amazement. Edward Kesselwood, the scientist who had served under General Axford in the Gulf War? But surely he was dead?

'Emmanuel Kimber!' Kesselwood recognised the man. He ripped off his mask and Colette turned her head away in horror. The whole of White Mask's lower face was burnt and scarred.

'Our agents thought you were dead,' Kimber said.

'I was left for dead, when my plane crashed in the desert,' Kesselwood said. The local people rescued me, and did their best for me. But they could not save my face.'

'And so that's who you're working for now?' Kimber asked.

'You know that the Project is above politics. It works for no country or nation.' Kesselwood said. He looked around at the ruins of the convent. 'It amused me to set up my base of operations here, right under the Institute.'

'It's the obvious place,' Kimber said. 'It's the spot where a number of ley-lines cross.'

'And also the place run by Axford,' Kesselwood said, pronouncing the name with disgust. 'The General who dismissed me from the service and sent me off in that doomed plane.'

'Give me the American boy,' Kimber said. 'It's the end of the road for you now, Kesselwood.'

Kesselwood moved backwards towards the command console, all the while keeping his eyes on Kimber and his revolver. He reached behind his back and operated a control. On the bench Joey's body convulsed with pain.

'No! Don't make me do it!' Joey cried. He struggled to free himself from the leather straps.

'You *shall* serve the Project!' Kesselwood snarled. He adjusted more controls on the command console.

Kreeee . . .

Sweat was pouring down Joey's brow now. His eyes were scrunched together in pain.

'My head hurts!' he screamed. 'Don't make me do it!'
Kreeee . . .

Marc, Rebecca and Colette watched on in horror, as Kimber staggered to the ground. He was already dripping with sweat and he was clutching his middle in pain. He glanced up at Kesselwood, pleading with him to stop the agonies that were building up inside his belly. Kesselwood laughed.

What happened next would remain with Marc, Rebecca, Colette and Joey for the rest of their lives. There was a singeing smell in the air, and they saw Kimber's white hair darken as the invisible energies conjured up by Joey started to consume his entire body.

Kimber's face started to blacken and he raised his hands to his eyes. When he brought them down again, there were no eyes. Just two empty sockets, filled with cinders.

The skin started to peel away from his body. Now the room was filled with the dreadful cloying stench of burning flesh. Kimber opened his charred mouth – but no sound came, for his lungs could no longer take in air. In fact, he no longer had any lungs.

And then there was a flash, and Kimber was gone. All that remained of him was a pile of ashes and his hands – which turned Rebecca's stomach most of all.

'An effective little device, isn't it?' Kesselwood chuckled. 'The Williams child taps into the ley-forces of the earth and trains them on to whatever or whoever I choose.'

'You monster!' Colette exclaimed. 'You made Joey kill him!'

'Of course I did,' Kesselwood answered nonchalantly. 'As I shall make him kill any who stand in the way of the Project.'

'What is the Project?' Marc demanded once again.

'That's no concern of yours, especially as you are all about to die.'

Help us, Joey! Please!

'You can't do this!' Rebecca said.

'Just try me.'

Colette took a step forward. 'If you kill them, I won't help you,' she said defiantly.

'Help me? What are you talking about, girl?'

'I've got the same powers as Joey,' she told him.

'Colette, voices in your head aren't the same thing,' Rebecca whispered.

'Why do you think it was me who heard them, and never you or Marc?' Colette said. 'Joey reached out to the only mind that was compatible with his.'

Kesselwood considered the matter for a moment. Perhaps the girl was telling the truth. But her abilities were nothing compared to those of Joey.

He shook his head. 'The gains would be too little from a mind like yours,' he said. 'Even with the Williams child we had to arrange for a trauma to awaken his sleeping psychic powers.'

'A trauma?' asked Marc.

'Two in fact.' Kesselwood smiled at the memory. 'It was when one of our agents pointed out to us that she knew a boy who displayed great psychic potential.'

'Agent?' Joey was intrigued, in spite of himself.

'The Project employs millions world-wide to spy

on their neighbours,' Kesselwood continued. 'Any piece of information, no matter how small, is recorded and acted upon.'

Joey remembered Old Mother Henshaw in the apartment downstairs back in Harlem, how she had always spooked him with her snooping ways. Had she told the Project about him?

'So a murder was arranged on the streets of New York,' Kesselwood recalled. 'And when even that trauma was insufficient to spark his talents into being, a little road accident was planned. His sister's death shocked him so much that they brought out his latent abilities.'

'You killed my sister and my mom!'

'Of course.'

The realisation devastated Joey. Kesselwood and the Project had killed the two people in the world who had ever mattered to him. Just so that they could use him in their filthy experiments to create the Mindfire. He hated Kesselwood and the Project with all his heart. He hated them with all the powers that Sara's and his mom's death had awoken in him.

Something in Joey snapped. He screamed out in anger. Tears poured freely from his eyes. His mind raged against the helmet he wore on his head. He refused to accept its power over him any longer.

The computers along the wall exploded in a shower of sparks and flames; the monitor screens cracked. There was a deep rumbling in the bowels of the earth, and Kesselwood and the others almost lost their balance as the ground swayed to and fro.

Kreeee . . .

In the centre of the chamber a great ball of fire appeared, much bigger than any before. It was Joey, calling up the powers of the earth itself. Slowly it grew in size, until it was threatening to fill the entire room.

'He's channelling too much power through himself!' Kesselwood realised. 'He won't be able to control it!'

Kesselwood and Omar raced towards the stone door at the far end of the chamber. Marc started to run after them, but was stopped by Rebecca.

'We have to get him out of here!' she said as she started to unfasten Joey's leather straps, and Colette took off the helmet.

'They killed my sister and my mom,' Joey said as Marc helped him to sit up. 'I can't take it any longer . . .'

Marc looked at the fireball. It was several times larger than it had been just seconds ago. The heat was becoming intense, unbearably so. It was getting hard to breathe as the Mindfire started to burn up the oxygen in the air itself. Marc's hands started to tingle, and his flesh began to scorch. Soon it would be too late for any of them. 'That thing's going to reach critical mass any moment now,' said Marc. 'We've got to get out.'

'The way Kesselwood took,' Rebecca asked Joey. 'Where does it lead to?'

'Who cares where it leads to?' Marc said sensibly and pulled Joey to his feet. 'Let's just get out of here!'

Kreeee . . .

They raced out of the chamber the way Kesselwood had gone, and found themselves in the large tunnel, which Joey had taken when he'd escaped. Behind them they could feel the fire growing wilder. They felt dizzy from the heat and lack of oxygen.

They raced as fast as their legs could take them, until they reached a second stone door. Not bothering where it might lead to, Marc pushed them all through, just as the fireball down in Kesselwood's underground lab reached its maximum size, and exploded.

Dateline: Saint Michael's Churchyard; Beltane; 00.22.

The blast threw them all four of them face down on to wet grass. They looked behind them. They had emerged from a stone tomb in the graveyard of Saint Michael's church. Smoke was billowing out of the open doorway, stinging their noses and eyes. It rose into the air, obscuring the full moon, and the lightning which forked in the Beltane sky.

A little way off, the windows of Saint Michael's church had been shattered by the explosion, and part of one of the outer walls had been broken by the force of the blast.

'It's one of Kimber's sacred ley-line sites, then,' Marc realised. 'To think that Kesselwood's secret lab was underneath Saint Michael's all the time.'

'Where's Kesselwood?' Colette asked. 'And his henchman?'

'Who cares?' Rebecca said. 'Joey's safe now and the machine is destroyed.'

'We still don't know what the Project is,' Marc said. He stood up and walked to that part of the church wall which had been nearest the blast. Some bricks had been loosened by the force of the explosion, and he began to remove them one by one.

'How are you feeling, Joey?' Colette asked.

'I've got the mother of all headaches,' the New York kid quipped, even though his eyes were still full of tears at the memory of his mother and Sara's deaths. 'Say, do you think I'll be able to whip up any more of those fireballs?'

'Not without Kesselwood's machine,' Rebecca said. 'And that will be well and truly buried now. But you've obviously got some kind of powerful psychic powers. Maybe we should study you at the Institute!'

'Hey, I'm not being no human guinea pig!' Joey cried.

'I thought you said that you didn't believe in para-normal powers,' Colette reminded Rebecca.

'I believe my own eyes,' Rebecca said. 'And trust me, what I've seen with them tonight takes some believing!' She looked over at Marc, who had managed to remove several more bricks from the wall. 'What do you think you're doing?' she asked. 'We don't want to cause any more damage than we already have!'

'There's something here,' Marc said as he levered out another brick from the wall. 'Hand me your torch, Bec.'

Rebecca handed him the torch and Marc shone its light into the space he had uncovered. She jumped back, more in surprise than in horror.

A skull was grinning back at her. The skull was attached to a skeleton, and around its neck there hung a silver crucifix.

'Sister Uriel!' Marc grinned. 'There, Bec. She really did exist. And we've finally found her!'

Dateline: The Institute; Friday 12th May; 02.30.

From his vantage point at the top of Saint Michael's church, Edward Kesselwood looked down as the fire engine and the police cars finally left Saint Michael's church.

He had chosen to hide in the church's belltower until all the commotion had died down, and, as he watched the rain batter down on the ground below, he wondered what had happened to Omar. As soon as they had escaped from the lab he had gone running off on his own.

Kesselwood laughed to himself. He didn't need Omar, just as he hadn't really needed that nurse, Maria. Omar was little more than a hired thug, and Maria had been so simple-minded that she'd believed him when he'd told her that he was developing the Mindfire machine for peaceful purposes.

He didn't even need the Project. No, all that mattered was Edward Kesselwood. One day he would rebuild the Mindfire, and finally get his revenge on Axford and his accursed Institute.

A soft footfall behind him made him turn and he raised his gun at the new arrival.

'You have disappointed the Project,' the Deputy Controller of the Project stated flatly.

'It wasn't my fault,' Kesselwood claimed. 'The child was too unstable, too angry. We couldn't control his powers.'

'You were employed by the Project to use the boy's abilities to develop the Mindfire weapon,' the Deputy Controller continued in an emotionless voice. 'That was your purpose. Your purpose is at an end.'

'Omar? Where is Omar?'

'Dead,' came the Deputy Controller's emotionless reply. Kesselwood had a very good idea who had killed him.

The Deputy Controller of the Project was approaching, and Kesselwood backed away. Even though he had a gun in his hand, he was unable to pull the trigger. His hands were shaking too much. Of all the men and women who worked for the Project, this was the one he feared the most.

'Please, keep away from me,' he said. He backed out towards the door which led out on to the church roof.

'Your purpose is at an end.' It was Kesselwood's death sentence.

They were now out on the church roof, in the middle of the storm. Rain lashed Kesselwood's face; the wind nearly made him lose his balance. He could hear the roar of thunder. Lightning streaked through the coal-black sky.

Still the Deputy Controller advanced on Kessel-wood, who was now standing near the edge of the roof. He summoned up all his courage and aimed his gun.

'You will not shoot me.'

Kesselwood knew that was the truth. There was something about the Deputy Controller's eyes. Even beneath those dark glasses, they carried a power, an authority that was . . . well, that was almost *unearthly*.

Kesselwood felt himself losing his balance. The Deputy Controller drew nearer to him. Kesselwood's arms flailed about and he grabbed the only means of support he could see.

The moment Edward Kesselwood touched the lightning conductor of Saint Michael's church, a bolt of lightning crackled out of the sky, setting his entire body aflame. Just as Joey had become a conductor for the hidden powers of the earth, so Kesselwood became a conductor for the fire of the heavens.

Unfortunately, for Kesselwood, he couldn't channel the lightning through his own body the way Joey could. He tumbled to the ground some thirty metres below – a smoking, fiery corpse.

Up on the church roof the Deputy Controller of the Project looked down. Death was the way in which she always liked these affairs to end. It solved so many problems, she thought.

Smiling to herself, she made her way back down to the Institute.

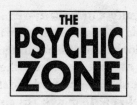

Epilogue

Dateline: The Institute; Friday 11th May; 12.30

'They don't believe us! Nobody believes us!' Marc said when he met up with the others the next day during the lunch break.

'Why would Ashby and his cops down at the station believe such a crazy story, Marc?' Rebecca asked.

'We all saw it with our own eyes, Bec,' he reminded her. 'But they think we're just a bunch of crazy kids wasting police time.'

'Joey was kidnapped,' Colette said. 'They can't deny that.'

'Don't you believe it!' Marc said angrily. 'They said that if we wanted to make a complaint then we would have to refer it to "higher authority".'

'The Project has got to them as well,' Joey said. 'Just as it got to the NYPD when Mom and Sara died and they wouldn't look into their murders.'

'At least Joey can take his place at the Institute now,' Rebecca said. 'And Miss Rumford and the local history group are delighted we've uncovered Uriel's skeleton.'

'Not that delighted,' Colette pointed out. 'The explosion from Kesselwood's machine made the tunnel cave in. There's no trace now of the old abbey. Or the Project.'

'So it's just as if the Mindfire never existed,' Marc said angrily. 'The Project again.'

'What do you think the Project is, Marc?' Joey asked.

'Who knows?' Marc said. 'But why do I think Eva's involved with it somehow? Maybe Axford as well.'

'You've no proof,' Rebecca reminded him.

'Kesselwood had to get that equipment underground somehow,' Marc said. 'Remember when Eva gave us those two days' holiday? Maybe she called that so none of us would be around when the equipment was delivered?'

'And maybe she didn't,' Rebecca said. 'And maybe she discovered the existence of the buried abbey when building work started on the kitchen annexe.'

'And maybe she didn't,' Marc repeated. 'She's covered her tracks too well.'

'These are only theories, Marc,' Rebecca continued. 'We need hard, firm evidence.'

'I know,' Marc said determinedly. 'And that's what

we're going to find. All four of us. Something's going on at the Institute that I don't like. And we'll discover what it is, if it's the last thing we do!'